Loving My Wicked Rogue

Loving My Wicked Rogue

SCANDALOUS GENTLEMEN BOOK ONE

DAWN BROWER

Contents

EXCERPT: THE RAKE WHO
LOVES ME

EXCERPT: COURTING A
CHRISTMAS WALLFLOWER

This is a work of fiction. Names, characters, places, and incidents are products of the author's imagination or are used fictitiously and are not to be construed as real. Any resemblance to actual locales, organizations, or persons, living or dead, is entirely coincidental.

Loving My Wicked Rogue © 2022 Dawn Brower

Cover art by Midnight Muse

For all those that find strength when they need it most. Do not give up. You never know what you might discover in the middle of your journey.

You must be the best judge of your own happiness.

— JANE AUSTEN, EMMA

Prologue

December 1865

Lady Francesca Kendall stared at the Christmas decoration she'd made, and frowned. It was lovely to spend time with her cousin, Lady Adeline Carwyn. They were only a few years apart in age. Francesca had turned eight and ten a few months prior, and Adeline was three years older than her. Christmastide was being celebrated at Whitewood Abbey, Adeline's home, or more accurately the home of her parents the Duke and Duchess of Whitewood. Adeline's mother was Francesca's father's sister. They were close, and had a celebration with their entire family every Christmas.

"What do you think of this?" Francesca asked. She held up a star that she'd colored a pale yellow. It was plain, simple, and in her opinion, elegant. That was how Francesca hoped to present herself to the ton during her first season. She would have her comeout ball in March when the season started. She couldn't wait until she could attend balls, soirees, garden parties, and more. Francesca couldn't understand why Adeline hated them so much.

"It is quite lovely," Adeline said. "It'll make a nice addiction to the tree when we decorate it tomorrow." She held up her own ornament and asked, "Do you think it is too much?" She was painting an angel in a circular piece of clay. It was exquisite.

"Oh…" She nibbled on her bottom lip and looked back at her star. Maybe she could do better. "You are so talented. I wish I had…something." Francesca was terrible at the pianoforte, mediocre at drawing and watercolors, and abysmal at needlepoint. In short, she had more failings than winsome attributes.

"Do not be that way," Adeline said. Her tone

held a hint of chastisement. "You're brilliant, beautiful, and the very epitome of benevolence." She smiled softly. "And I love you. I do not want to listen to you berate yourself, or what you believe to be your lack of marketable traits."

She pasted a smile on her face. Francesca didn't particularly feel pretty or desirable. Perhaps that would change after her comeout. She prayed she wouldn't become a wallflower, or a spinster like Adeline. Francesca wanted to find love and have a marriage like her parents had. They loved each other so much it almost hurt to watch them. How possible was it for her to find a love as special and strong as theirs? "I'll try, it's all I can promise." She glanced away and started to add more flourish to her star. If Adeline could create something as special as an angel ornament, surely she could make something equally as pretty. Adeline stood and wiped her hands on her apron.

"Are you already finished," Francesca asked. "I'm not nearly done."

"I am." She smiled at her. "I'm weary and am going to lie down until dinner." She did appear a bit fatigued. "When you're done do not forget to wash and change. You have a bit of paint in your hair and on your hands. You probably brushed your hand over your hair."

Adeline glanced at her hands and frowned. She did have paint all over her hands and the apron she wore over her gown. Francesca stared down at herself. "I will, thank you." She should be more careful, but part of her didn't care. She'd been trying to be creative after all.

"Will you be joining us for tea?" Francesca asked. She brushed a lock of her strawberry blonde hair behind an ear. Sometimes she wished she had golden blonde hair like Adeline. Her reddish locks were not nearly as fashionable. There was so much about herself she wished she could change, but accepted she couldn't. Francesca needed to stop comparing herself to Adeline. It would lead her nowhere. All the negativity did not do any good, and she loved her cousin. She wouldn't hurt her for anything and yet, she couldn't stop being a brat, at least in her mind.

"I am uncertain," she told her nonchalantly. "But don't expect me. I may stay in my chambers longer depending on how I feel."

"All right," Francesca said absentmindedly. Francesca had turned her attention back to her ornament already, and frowned again. Maybe she'd do an outline in another color. She wasn't certain how to make it stand out. "Have a nice rest."

"I will," Adeline told her and then smiled softly. "Do not fret. Your ornament really is quite lovely." With those words Adeline left Francesca alone. She painted a thin dark yellow outline and considered it good. Perhaps Adeline was right. It was beautiful and she should stop doubting herself. She carried it over to the table to dry. They'd add ribbon to their ornaments before putting them on the tree.

Adeline cleaned up her supplies, and then left the craft room. As she was rounding the corner to go up to her bedchamber she stumbled against a man. She mumbled her apologies before she glanced up. Her mouth went dry and she lost all ability to think, let alone speak. He had thick black hair, and eyes so blue they took her breath away. In short, she was a bumbling mess. Francesca had never seen a man as beautiful as this one, and had nothing to fall back on in her interaction with him.

"No need to apologize," he said in a husky tone. She'd somehow managed to find her breath, and shivers went down her spine as he spoke. God help her. "It was all my fault." He had so much charm no lady would be able to resist. Who was he?

She shook her head still unable to speak. What

was wrong with her? So he was gorgeous. That shouldn't matter! If she had any chance of having a successful season she had to learn to use her voice. "My lord," she curtsied. "It was indeed my fault. I cannot let you take the blame."

His lips tilted upward into a sinful smile that promised he could be quite wicked if a lady let him have his way with her. Francesca had never been so tempted to offer herself to a man before. But to be fair, no men like this one lived near her home in Kent. "A gentleman would never let a lovely lady as you carry such a burden." He held out his hand to her. "Why don't you stroll with me. I'm only here until morning and I find myself a bit lonely."

She frowned. Francesca should help out and spend some time with him. This was her aunt's house, and she did know the layout, and what might appeal to him. "I am afraid we've not been introduced…"

"Then let's rectify that." He brought her hand up to his lips and pressed down in a soft kiss. "I am Matthew."

That was not at all what she meant. Using his surname was absolutely scandalous, and she shouldn't do it. She tilted her head to the side and studied him. What did this man hope to achieve by being wicked with her? "Matthew?"

"Yes," that rich tone of his voice was a weapon and a gift. More importantly he seemed to understand that and used it to his advantage.

"Do you not believe it's too familiar?" He was an enigma. Why would he not want to know more about her, or her him?

"Not at all," he said smoothly Matthew stared intently into her eyes, and it made her want to believe everything he said to her. "I do believe you and I are destined to be…acquainted. Why stall the inevitable?"

Francesca barely held in a sigh. Was he right? Were they somehow meant to be? "I am Francesca," she acquiesced. "How do you feel about conservatories?"

"I love them," he said. "Is there one here? Will you show me?"

Francesca nodded. "The duchess has a lovely orange tree. It's one of the best conservatories in all of England, though perhaps not as wonderful as the one at Seabrook, I do love it."

He looped her arm with his. "Lead the way dear Cesca," he said in a tone so intimate it filled her with warmth. "And tell me about Seabrook. Have you visited there often?"

He didn't know who she was… Francesca smiled. She should tell him that the Marquess of Seabrook was her great uncle? Perhaps later. She liked this interaction with him and adored the shortened version of her name he used.

They reached the conservatory and Francesca was relieved no one else was there. That gave her more time alone with him. She led him to the orange tree. "Isn't it beautiful?"

"Not nearly as much as you are." She glanced at him and sucked in a breath. She may have never experienced desire, but she understood it existed. This man stared at her with so much need it made her insides quiver. She wanted him, and she decided she should have him.

"You say such sweet things Matthew." Her voice was soft and filled with the same need reflected in his eyes. "How sweet are you?"

"Let me show you," he said as he leaned down, and pressed his lips to hers.

The kiss was soft, coaxing, and as sweet as he promised. Then it turned into something much more passionate and consuming. He brought his hand up to her breast and dipped a finger underneath her bodice. He stroked her nipple and it hardened at his touch. The need between her thighs deepened and she didn't quite know what was happening.

He pushed the bodice down and lowered his head, sucked in that tight nipple, and she nearly screamed with pleasure. Sweet wasn't the right word. Matthew was a wicked rogue, and Francesca was falling in love with him. Nothing could stop the feelings spreading through her now.

He lifted her skirts and slid his hand between her thighs. She moaned as tiny quivers rocked her body. "You're so responsive," he whispered in her ear. "I want you." He groaned as he slid a finger inside her. She pressed herself against him. She wanted him to.

And she decided to give herself to him, body, soul, and especially, all the love in her heart… "Yes," she said. "Yes…" She promised herself she would not regret any of this. He was her destiny, and she'd never believed she'd be so lucky to find the man of her dreams before she started looking. Sometimes fate could be surprising in the best possible ways, and the pleasure Matthew made her feel…simply marvelous.

March 1866

Francesca was a fool… How could she have believed he loved her? She'd been hoping, and hoping for weeks now, and it was time to accept he didn't care for her at all. He'd seduced her, and it hadn't been particularly difficult either. She'd fallen willing into his arms and hadn't regretted that choice.

Until now…

She slid her hand down her belly and fought tears. Her dilemma could no longer be ignored. She had feared her condition and wished it away, but doing either didn't change anything. Francesca didn't know what to do. This was not a situation she'd ever believed she'd find herself in.

Her heart hurt. When Matthew hadn't come for her she should have realized then he'd used her. She'd made so many excuses for him, and she couldn't change that. She couldn't change any of it. If she wasn't facing the consequences of her choice she'd have eventually found a way to forget him, or at least not cry as much at the loss.

Francesca would like to believe she was smarter now, but there was no way to determine if she'd be so foolish over a man again. Her naivete had already came out shining on her first interaction with a handsome scoundrel. She wished she'd been at least smart enough to ask for his full name. Francesca wanted to slap him in the face for taking advantage of her.

Someone had to know who he was. He'd been at a family gathering after all. There were always more than family at Christmastide. They had friends of friends there. The question was how to discover his name without spilling her own secret along the way...

She sighed. It seemed too difficult. Matthew had been her downfall, and soon the entire ton would be able to see for themselves the mistake she'd made.

There was only so much time left before her belly gave it away. Even in that she wasn't certain how long it would be. She'd never been enceinte before…

"There you are," Scarlett Kendall, the Marchioness of Blackthorn, Francesca's mother said. "Why are you hiding out here?" Francesca inherited her strawberry blonde hair from her mother, though hers was lighter than her mother's richer red. The marchioness had hers pulled back into a simple plait, and her day dress, while elegant, was also a simple butter yellow with white lace trim around the bodice.

They had arrived in London earlier that week to prepare for the season. Her comeout ball would be in a couple of days. At first she'd been excited for it. Now she wished she could cancel it. Doing so would be a scandal in itself though, and she wouldn't add to her family's embarrassment. She'd sneaked out to the garden to find some peace from all the preparations. They had decided to stay at her grandfather, the Duke of Weston's, townhouse. The ballroom was larger and could accommodate the number of guests invited. After her ball they would retire to the smaller Blackthorn house.

"It's a lovely day don't you think?" It was actually quite chilly, but she'd needed the cooler air to help her overheated skin. She'd been ill at odd times of the day, and some days she seemed fine. At first she'd dismissed it as nerves. It wasn't until a couple days ago she'd realized she couldn't recall the last time her courses had come. "And there is so many people inside. It was stifling." That part was the complete truth. Francesca had heard balls were so packed sometimes it was difficult to move. That sounded almost terrifying now considering her condition.

"I'm sorry," her mother said. "Sometimes when one has to endure society obligations it can become unbearable." She lifted her hand and brushed a stray lock behind Francesca's ear. "But the good news is once this is done you can pick and choose what balls you wish to attend. Try to have fun."

Francesca wished and wished… But wishing didn't work. Her fate was already sealed. Since cancelling the ball was out of the question she'd see it through, and she would make a decision later what she should do next. She would like to at least attempt to uncover her baby's father's identity. If that wasn't possible then she'd confess all to her parents. She hoped it wouldn't come to that.

"I will have fun." She smiled, but she didn't feel

even the slightest bit happy. Francesca wondered if she would ever feel that way again. "I've been looking forward to this ball for a while now." And having her one night with Matthew had ruined it for her. "How could I not enjoy it. The preparations however…"

Her mother laughed. "They are tiresome." The smile fell from her mother's face. "Are you certain you are all right? I've been having strange dreams."

Francesca's heart raced. Her mother had a prognostic gift, and if she had dreams…they might give away her secret. "I'm fine." She put more effort into her smile. "I promise. What were these dreams about?"

Her mother glanced away. "They were flashes really. You didn't look happy, there was a man but I only saw him from the back. He had dark hair…" She shook her head. "It's probably nothing. Maybe he's the one you're meant to fall in love with. The path isn't always easy on the course to true love."

Her mother couldn't be more wrong. Matthew didn't love her at all, and even if she found him Francesca doubted he'd take responsibility for the baby he'd help create. Still she had to try..

"You could be right. The ball is soon, and

perhaps this mysterious man will be one of the guests."

Her mother hugged her. "I hope whoever the man is that wins your heart realizes how lucky he is to have you."

Francesca fought tears. Her voice was a little husky as she spoke, "I'm sure he will be worthy of it. I wouldn't pick a man undeserving now would I?"

"No you wouldn't," she agreed. Her mother pulled back then came to her feet. "Do not stay out here too long. It's too cold still." With those words she left Francesca alone with her thoughts once again…

MATTHEW GRANT, THE DUKE OF LINDSEY stared out the window in his study at his country estate, Lindy Castle. He'd grown up there. His parents had left him to the nanny's and governess's to raise. He didn't understand love, so it was no wonder he had been taken low by it when he was a green lad.

One lady, slightly older, and perhaps wiser had stolen his young heart and then crushed it cruelly. After that disastrous mistake he vowed never to give his heart to another. He had none to give either way, and now his heartless mother had decided it was time for him to marry. As if Matthew couldn't make a decision of his own.

If he wanted to marry there was one woman… He shook that thought away. Beautiful red haired beauties didn't belong in his world. He should never have had a taste of her innocence to begin with. He'd been a rotten bastard, and he laid awake many nights regretting making love to her. He couldn't go back and change it, and hell, he didn't really want to. She was the only good thing he'd had in his life and he wanted to cherish that memory.

"Are you listening to me?" Agatha, the Dowager Duchess of Lindsey demanded. His mother had finally realized that he'd stopped paying attention to her.

He took a sip of the brandy he held in his hand, then glanced briefly over his shoulder. "I do my best to never listen to you," he replied drolly. Why wouldn't she go away?

"You need to stop this roguish behavior. There are no heirs in the line of succession to the Lindsey title. If you don't marry and sire an heir…"

"The title will die with me." He rolled his eyes.

"I know this and do not need you to remind me of it." He turned around and strolled back to his desk, then lifted the decanter to refill his glass. "I don't bloody care if no one inherits the title. That seems far better than tying myself to a woman I'll hate."

"Once you have an heir you can ignore each other at your pleasure." His mother smiled. "It's an age old tradition."

"One you and my father did with aplomb." If his father hadn't died nearly ten years ago he'd probably be harassing Matthew too. "Forgive me if I do not wish to follow in your footsteps. I will not marry some cold society miss because you believe I need an heir."

His mother gasped. "Please tell me you do not have hopes to marry for love?"

Mathew burst into laughter. God help him. His mother was absolutely too much. "There is an appeal to that if you find it so offensive." He sipped more brandy. "However I believe in love less than I believe in marriage. It's a fantasy or for the very lucky." One of his friends was part of the latter. The Earl of Winchester had somehow miraculously found love over Christmastide. He didn't quite understand it. Love wasn't the norm, and as rare as it was, Matthew had no doubts he'd ever find it.

"Well at least you're not foolish enough to hold out for it." She brushed imaginary crumbs off her shoulder. "Now about your fiancée…"

"Bloody hell mother," he shouted at her as he slammed his glass on his desk. Brandy sloshed out and spilled over his hand. "I do not, nor will I ever have a damned fiancée. Stop this constant harping now."

"I'm not giving up on you marrying." She lifted her chin in defiance. "But I will give you some time to consider what I've said. The dukedom is important and I do hope you'll want to leave all of this to your son one day."

He opened his mouth to yell at her again, but then reconsidered and closed it. Arguing with his mother would not help his situation. She believed what she did, and he had his own opinions. It was far better to put some distance between them. "I won't change my mind." The muscles in his jaws twitched. "And I am done with this discussion." Somehow he managed to remain cool and composed.

"A duke doesn't have the choice to refrain from marriage. If you don't choose your bride, one will help you choose her. Mark my words."

A flash of his red haired beauty came to mind

again. He wanted her. Perhaps more than when he'd first met her. One taste hadn't been enough. Maybe he would try to find her again. If he were forced to have one woman as his wife she might do. No. He shook that thought away. He didn't want any bride…even her.

"You're wrong," he disagreed. "No woman will ever control me." He'd made that mistake once. Matthew learned from his mistakes. Edith Whitcomb had taught him that valuable lesson. When she shredded him with her machinations, and false love. She'd had him wrapped around her finger, and convinced him she'd make a wonderful wife. He'd been ready to run away with her before his father had stepped in. He'd offered her a better prize—an old duke and the title of duchess sooner than if she'd married him. Of course she couldn't have known Matthew's father would have a fatal accident a few months later. She could have had a younger husband, and the title too.

She deserved the bed she'd made for herself, and Matthew was free from ever marrying. His father had done him a favor, and he appreciated it, but not enough to finding a different bride. Even one as lovely as his Francesca. She would be far better off finding a gentleman worthy of her.

Matthew was rotten through and through, and he accepted that. "I'm happier alone."

"Keep telling yourself that," his mother said. "One day you might even believe it."

He turned toward her. His mother was a lovely woman with hair the same black as his own, but she had light green eyes. There was some gray streaked through her dark locks, but only enough to make her seem even lovelier. She must have been quite the beauty in her day. "I already do believe it."

With those words he left his unfinished brandy on his desk, then stalked out of the room. He would travel to London immediately. There at least he had his club for entertainments, and perhaps a whore or two to help him forget a woman he couldn't erase from his mind on his own.

When Francesca had woke up that morning she had to run to her wash-bowl as sickness overwhelmed her. Whatever had been left in her stomach had come back up. She'd never felt so miserable in her entire life. The very idea of food made her gag. She'd ordered tea and nothing else. The warmth liquid eased some of the queasiness in her stomach and by mid-morning she'd begun to feel almost normal again.

She held her hand over her stomach. The little baby growing inside of her was making itself known in the worst possible ways. She loved the child already and couldn't make herself completely regret his or her existence; however, that didn't negate her problem. She still needed a solution and had to find the baby's father to inform him of her condition. It was time to start that search and ask for help from the two people she trusted most with her secret—her two best friends, Violet and Iris Keene.

Francesca pulled the bell for her maid, Bess. She'd sent her away earlier when the very idea of rising for the day had seemed too tiresome. It didn't take long for Bess to walk into her bedchamber. She curtsied, "You need something my lady?"

"Yes," Francesca said. "I am ready to dress for the day." She slid out of bed. "I'm expected for tea at Dresden Manor." Francesca always went to visit her friends on Thursdays and was thankful this visit wouldn't be a surprise to anyone.

"Should you be going out when you are feeling unwell?" Bess asked. She tilted her head to the side. "You do seem to have some color back in your cheeks."

She hated lying to Bess, but she had no choice. "Whatever it was it passed quickly." Francesca lifted her lips into what she hoped was a cheerful smile. "I would hate to keep Iris and Violet waiting." She desperately needed to see the two of them and ask for their help. Surely one of them might know who Matthew was. If she explained it all to them and her urgency they'd help. They had always been there for her and they wouldn't let her down now. Francesca waited for Bess to retrieve the gown she'd planned to wear for her outing. They had discussed it the night before and Bess had taken it out to press. She'd returned it that morning when Francesca had been supposed to dress for the day. Since she hadn't felt well, Bess had hung it up.

The dress was a periwinkle that brought out the blue in Francesca's eyes. It was one of her favorite gowns, and she hoped it would make her feel pretty when she felt miserable at best. The sickness had passed; however, that didn't mean she was better. Tea was the only thing she had any desire to consume.

Bess came over to her side. "Let's get your stays tied now."

Francesca sucked in a breath as her maid pulled on the ribbons. "Not too tight," she said. "I would prefer to not add to my mishap from earlier." She wasn't certain how it might affect the baby, and she honestly didn't want to fight breathing and her illness. One at a time was all she could feasibly handle.

"Very well, my lady," Bess agreed. "You're quite right." After the stays were tied Bess helped her into her gown. "Now sit at the vanity so I can fix your hair."

"Nothing to elaborate," she told her. "I don't wish to have head pain either." Francesca didn't know having a baby growing inside her would cause so much calamity on her body. She thought the worst part would be the delivery, and she sure as hell wasn't looking forward to that part either.

Bess did a simple plait of Francesca's hair and then wound it into a knot at the base of her neck. Once it was pinned in place Bess declared, "There. You're ready for your visit now."

"Thank you." Francesca smiled. "I'll retrieve my wrap and walk to Dresden house. You do not need to accompany me today. It's not a far walk and I'd like some time alone."

"Very well, my lady." She curtsied. "Have a nice visit."

Francesca rushed down the stairs and was out of the house before anyone could stop her. She didn't want to run into her family. She set a brisk pace so she wouldn't be too late for tea. When she reached the Dresden house, she walked up the front steps and rapped the knocker against the door. After a few brief moments the door opened. The Dresden butler greeted her, "Welcome Lady

Francesca. Lady Violet and Lady Iris are waiting for you in the sitting room."

"Thank you, Barton," she said and then smiled. "I'll announce myself."

He bowed. "As you wish."

She was a frequent visitor and well acquainted with the household. Francesca rushed into the room and dropped into a chair across from Violet. Iris lounged on the settee. Iris and Violet were fraternal twins. Both had golden blond hair, but Iris had grass green eyes, and Violet sea-green ones.

"We were beginning to wonder if you forgot about us," Violet said. "Why are you so late?"

Iris poured a cup of tea and fixed it how Francesca liked it, then handed it to her. "Here you go dear. You look as if you need it."

"I do?" She lifted a brow. Francesca didn't disagree with her, but she hadn't realized she gave off that impression.

"Yes," Violet said and studied her. "You appear a bit piqued. What is going on with you?"

Francesca sighed then took a sip of her tea. This was the difficult part. She had to unburden herself and she hoped they wouldn't think less of her. Her hand shook a little as she settled the teacup on the saucer. "I need your help."

"Of course," Iris said in a calm, reassuring tone. "We will do anything for you."

She stared at her tea. Where should she start? "Do you recall my family's Christmastide celebration?"

They had both been there for at least half of the time. This was why she hoped they could help her. Violet nodded. "It was memorable. Why are you asking us this?"

She blew out a breath. Before she told them about her condition she had to know if they knew Matthew's full identity. "Do you recall a man with ink black hair and deep blue eyes. He had a slight dimple in his left cheek."

Iris frowned. "Do you mean the Duke of Lindsey?"

"I'm not certain. Do you know his given name?"

Violet tilted her head to the side. "I believe I do. It's…Matthew. My mother is acquainted with his and once I overheard her complaining about her son and his unwedded state. I believe her words were something to the affect 'Matthew refuses to marry and provide the dukedom with an heir. There has to be a way to make that rotten boy see reason.'"

"Why do you want to know about the duke?" Iris asked. "I do hope you haven't set your cap for him. He's completely against marriage." There was concern etched through her voice.

She held her hand over her stomach and swallowed the lump in her throat. "Well, I'm going to have to change his mind." Then she proceeded to explain to them her dilemma. It was one of the hardest things she'd ever done; however, she fully expected telling Matthew, followed by her parents, would be inherently worse. After she was done explaining it to her friends it had helped her to devise a plan. It would be best to contact the duke in private first and hope he would do the honorable thing. If he refused…they'd rethink how he should be approached. With an idea of what she should do Francesca felt truly better for the first time that day. She had to believe it would all be settled soon.

Matthew sat in the study at the London townhouse. It was inherently more peaceful without his mother constantly harping on him. He closed his eyes and enjoyed the peace surrounding him. This was the best part of being the Duke of Lindsey. He owned so many properties it was easy enough to find one his mother didn't reside in if necessary. He opened his eyes and smiled. His friend the Marquess of Merrifield leaned against the door frame with an amused grin on his face. His dark hair was quite mussed, and his blue eyes nearly twinkled with mischief. His clothing was disheveled as if he didn't have a valet skilled in keeping his clothing tidy.

"A little birdie informed me you were in town," Merrifield said from the entrance to the study.

He chuckled lightly. "That explains your ragged appearance." Matthew quirked a brow and drawled, "Am I acquainted with this birdie?"

"It's a possibility," Merrifield answered. "She is the more…risqué sort. From what I understood she saw your carriage roll into town while she paid a call on one of her more exclusive clients."

"Would that client happen to be a marquess that resembles you?" Matthew held back a smile. He had a feeling he knew exactly what birdie he referred to.

"I admit nothing." He held up his hand. "Except I do enjoy the more carnal pleasures in life."

"As do I," Matthew agreed. This time he did

smile. "How is the fair Esmée?" She was one of London's notorious courtesans. She didn't have many clients, but the ones she did were the amongst the wealthiest, and more elite titles. Matthew used to be amongst them until he had decided she bored him. After that he didn't bed the same woman twice and had become more selective in the ones he did enjoy. He was actually in a bit of a dry spell. Matthew hadn't found a woman that appealed to him since Christmas. He was having a lot of trouble shaking his need for his red haired Cesca.

"Esmée is doing quite well. She said to tell you she misses you."

Matthew rolled his eyes. "I bet she does." She probably missed his money and extravagant gifts. He certainly didn't miss her. Once he decided to dismiss a lady, he didn't give them a second chance, and Esmée was no lady. "I however want something a little less used." That was perhaps a bit crude, but the truth. He was done with whores. Perhaps he could find a nice widow to seduce. That might help him forget Cesca.

"Suit yourself," Merrifield said. "You usually do."

"You speak the truth." Matthew went to the bar near his desk. "Would you care for a brandy?"

"I could drink a glass or two," Merrifield replied.

Matthew poured them each two fingers of brandy. He handed a snifter to Merrifield and then settled down on one of the mahogany chairs in the study. He sipped on his brandy and enjoyed the burn as it traveled down his throat. "Now tell me why you're here."

"I cannot visit a friend without having a reason?"

"No," Matthew said in a clipped tone. "You have an agenda of some sort. Tell me."

"It's nothing." He sighed. "I'm feeling a bit of ennui." He settled into the other chair. "Hampstead and Goodland are still at their country seats. I don't expect they'll be in town soon and I was relieved to hear you'd returned earlier than expected." He blew out a breath. "Please tell me that you have some entertainments scheduled."

He didn't. "My return was rather spontaneous. I have no specific plans." He took another drink of brady. "I expect if we can discern a spot of fun if we think about it. But not tonight. I want to relax after the journey to town. Come back tomorrow and we will combine our considerable resources toward debauchery and scandal."

Merrifield grinned, then swallowed his brandy in one gulp. "I knew I could count on you." He set his empty glass down. "I'll let you recuperate from your journey. Until tomorrow…" He got up to leave.

When he reached the door. "Merrifield," he called out.

The marquess glanced over his shoulder. "Yes?"

"Next time don't dishonor the brandy. It is meant to be savored. Like you would pleasure a lady. It's best enjoyed in slow succulent measures."

Merrifield laughed. "Not all ladies need that kind of loving. Sometimes a good hard round brings more pleasure than soft kisses and promises that will be broken in the end."

"True enough," he said then grinned. "However, my brandy isn't a whore like you've become accustomed to."

Merrifield's laughter echoed back at him as he walked down the hall and left Matthew on his own. Now that he was alone again, he'd find that peace he desperately needed.

Three

The visit with Violet and Iris had gone well. Francesca had a plan. It wasn't necessarily guaranteed to be successful, but at least she had something to work toward. Matthew would be surprised. Probably not about his impending fatherhood… The more she learned about the depraved duke she'd begun to wonder what she'd seen in him that night. He'd been so charming, but that was part of his act. He acted as if the woman he kissed and loved was the only one that made his heart beat. It had been…affective. Francesca had fallen for every word, every touch, and every single insincere promise.

And if he tossed her aside, she'd be ruined forever…

Not that she wasn't already, but at least if he did the honorable thing no one had to know about her indiscretion. She did not have a good feeling about what he might do. Francesca fully believed he'd laugh at her and show her the door. If he even allowed her inside his home…

She swallowed hard. No matter how terrified she felt she could not let that stop her from trying. She had made the decision to be with him and confronting him was part of those consequences. Francesca intended to do that after dark. Once her parents retired for the evening she'd sneak out and walk to his townhouse. As luck would have it, he lived nearby or at least the townhouse he owned in London was on the same street. She couldn't be certain he was in town, but she hoped her luck, at least in telling him about the baby, held. Everything else had not been so fortuitous.

"You're not eating," her mother said. "Are you still a little under the weather?"

Francesca pushed around the potatoes on her plate. She'd been wishing dinner was over so she could excuse herself. "I am not hungry." She smiled hoping it eased her mother's concern. "I think I'm over whatever ailed me earlier." And she was…at least until morning. She had a feeling her sickness would be back. Francesca had to find a way to hide that from her parents. Her mother would discern the truth about her condition if the entire household was aware, she became sick each morning. That was another reason to see the duke as soon as possible. Matthew had to take responsibly. Just had to... If he didn't, she'd have to face her parents and accept her reputation was in tatters.

"I hope so. Your maid said you were miserable. I'm glad you didn't suffer too long with it." Her mother picked up her glass of wine and sipped. "Perhaps you would like to accompany me on a visit to the modiste. We can order you some more gowns."

"I don't need any new gowns." At least not yet... When she grew rounder, she'd have to get some new ones. "I might visit Aunt Elizabeth. Didn't she arrive in town today?" Her aunt had a gift of sight too, and if Matthew turned her away, she might need some guidance. "and Adeline should be here soon too with her new husband."

"I have some business to discuss with your Uncle Jack," her father told her. "You can ride over with me if you want. I'm going early though."

She didn't know how much sleep she'd manage after her visit with Matthew, but a ride with her father would be preferable than walking. "That would be lovely," Francesca replied. "I'll have Bess wake me early enough to accompany you."

Dinner seemed to go on forever, but it did eventually come to an end. Francesca excused herself and went to her bedchambers. She didn't ring for Bess. She'd told her maid earlier not to come up and to take the night off. When she'd dressed for dinner, she had Bess help her into a gown that didn't require stays and buttoned up the front. She had to be able to undress herself after she returned home, and she didn't want her maid to grow suspicious. This way Bess was grateful for an evening to herself and didn't question it. Especially as it wasn't the first time, she'd done something similar.

Francesca paced her bedchamber until she thought it was safe enough to sneak off. She grabbed her cloak, donned it, then pulled the hood up over her head. She went down the servants' stairs and out the back door. The servants had all retired for the evening. There was a slight chance her parents were still awake, and she didn't want to risk going out the front door. She walked down the street quickly. Francesca glanced back several times. Her heart raced heavily as she moved toward Matthew's townhouse.

Finally, she reached the door. She stared at it uncertain what to do next. The duke wouldn't answer his own door. He'd have servants for that, and what if they turned her away? There was always that possibility and she should have considered it. Francesca took a deep breath and then went up the stairs. When she reached the door, she lifted the knocker and rapped it three times against the door. She held her breath and waited for it to open. Several seconds went by and she blew out that breath when the door creaked open.

She was shocked to her core when Matthew actually opened the door. Her mouth fell open and she couldn't speak for so long it seemed as if time had frozen still. His dark hair was disheveled, and his eyes had a glassy appearance to them. He lifted a brow. "Go ahead and speak I don't have all night."

Francesca found her composure and lowered the hood of her cloak. Surprise filled his eyes, but it was brief. She lifter her gaze to meet his and boldly said, "Your Grace, let me come inside."

She didn't think he'd let her inside, but then he held the door open wider. Francesca slid past him into his foyer. Now the hard part would begin…

MATTHEW DIDN'T KNOW WHY SHE WAS AT HIS HOME, and part of him had thought he'd imagined her; however, he couldn't be happier she'd found him. Perhaps it was time to have her a second time and erase her from his mind once and for all. She'd been haunting him for too long.

He shut the door and turned to her. Matthew lifted his lips into a sensual smile. "Why hello, Cesca."

"So, you remember me?" She tilted her head to the side. "I had wondered if you would, considering your lecherous habits." She didn't sound at all happy to see him…which only proved to confuse him further.

Damn if she wasn't even more beautiful than he remembered though. Her strawberry blonde hair glowed in the candlelight, a few strands had come loose from the plait, and her blue eyes had fire in them. She was angry. That only made her more appealing to him. "How could I forget you." He stalked forward. "It was bold of you to seek me out at home. Normally that would be something I'd find unforgiveable, but with you I'm willing to make an exception."

He needed her naked and moaning underneath him. Their one night together had been too fast, and she had been mostly clothed. He could rectify that mistake now. Perhaps that was why he couldn't forget her. Matthew hadn't had ample opportunity to taste every inch of her delectable skin. He wanted to kiss her until she screamed his name, then he'd plunge inside of her and ride her until she screamed it again.

Bloody hell he was hard already. He might have to keep her with him all night. Once wasn't going to be enough. Matthew would need hours with her to get his fill. He studied her as she did the same with him. What was the chit after?

"I do not care if you find my presence unforgiveable or not," she replied scathingly. "If I had a choice, I wouldn't be here at all. The sight of you make me sick, but then again, a lot does these days."

"I'm afraid I'm not following you." He quirked a brow. "If you don't wish to see me, why are you here?"

She did seem rather irate. There was a little pink in her cheeks, and her hands were fisted at er sides. Matthew was glad he'd given his staff the night off. He'd done it when he'd had other ideas for the night, but those had fallen through. Since she was always on his mind, the whores he'd hoped to use to forget her were supposed to spend the evening with him. Matthew had sent them away before they could even really begin. He couldn't get hard for them, but his lovely Cesca stepped in front of him, and he'd been ready to rut for hours. What the blazes was wrong with him?

"Why did you never pay a call on me?" Her lips wobbled a little as she spoke. "After that night…" She shook her head. "I thought you wanted more with me. I realize now it was a foolish girl's hopes, but I want you to tell me. I need to hear it."

"Ah," he said softly. "I should have expected this." He sighed. "Why don't we go into the sitting room. We shouldn't stand in the foyer conversing."

Matthew didn't know what to tell her. The trek to the sitting room was his way of stalling the inevitable. Perhaps he could find some pretty words to tell her. When he'd started to kiss her, he'd discovered her sweetness, and suspected her innocence, but couldn't stop himself. He'd wanted her like he had never wanted anything in his entire life, and he didn't regret that night. She was a siren to him.

She followed him into the sitting room, and then he gestured for her to sit on the settee. He debated if he should sit next to her or in the chair. If he sat beside her, she would prove too much of a temptation. He'd kiss her and then they'd be exactly where they were now. Matthew decided to sit in the chair. It was for the best. She seemed distraught and he didn't want to add to it. If she joined him in his bed again, he wanted it to be her decision. He wouldn't seduce her this time.

"So?" She folder her hands in her lap. "Tell me."

"I…" How did he say this without making everything worse? "I should apologize. I could say some pretty words and make excuses, but the truth is there is none. I don't get involved with women more than one night. It's how it's always been."

"And you believe that makes it all right?" She pursed her lips in displeasure. "You use women because you believe they are there for your pleasure. Do you not consider the consequences of the blatant disregard you have for females?"

He sighed. God help him. Matthew hated

confrontations with women. They could be so hysterical and trying. Though most of them demanded money. Thankfully, he had plenty and he could hand it to them and wave them off. None of them had ever returned again. Though admittedly until Cesca they'd all been servants, or women of ill repute. He had never dallied with anyone of quality. That should have said something to him and explained a little why he couldn't forget about her. "I've never left a woman unsatisfied." He tilted his lips upward into an arrogant half-smile. "In or out of bed."

"I wouldn't know," she retorted. "We never shared a bed." Cesca looked at him from top to bottom. "And out of one I can honestly say I've been quite disappointed."

Matthew chuckled. She was perfect, and he would have her naked and underneath him. She didn't realize it, but she'd just challenged him, and he never backed down from one before, and he wouldn't start with her. "I can rectify that."

"Charming," she said. So much sarcasm filled that one word it was razor sharp as if it might draw blood as it slid out of her mouth. "But I am afraid I must decline your offer. I didn't come here for a repeat performance. The last time was a mistake, and I have the unwelcome gift you left to prove it." She held her hand over her stomach, and it was like she punched him in his. Nothing could have shocked him more. He had to have mistaken her intent. She couldn't be…

Four

So many emotions crossed over his face as he took in her words. It was almost entertaining to watch. First shock, then denial, followed quickly by anger. His cheeks were now flushed a bright red, and his hands had curled into fists. Francesca didn't think he'd hurt her, but she couldn't be certain. She prayed she hadn't made a mistake coming to see him alone.

"I don't believe you," he said in a defiant tone. "Whatever you are hoping to gain by lying to me now…it will not work. You can crawl back under the hole you were buried in. I am not claiming any brat you might be carrying. If you are enceinte, and I doubt you are, it is not my child."

Francesca sighed. She wished she had expected

a different response, but she hadn't. A man who seduced an innocent girl and then abandoned her would not take responsibility for his actions. She really had a terrible judge of character, and the bad taste to fall in love with a reprobate. The sad truth was she did indeed still harbor feelings for him. She wished she didn't but for whatever reason her stubborn heart wouldn't let go of hope he felt the same way about her.

"Hole?" She lifted a brow. "You think I am some poor relation that everyone takes pity on." Francesca stood and faced him. "Why would you ever believe such a thing? As if I'm not worthy of your, or anyone's attention." Anger pierced her soul and she never wanted to punch a person as much as she did him. "This child, and much to my dismay, yes, there is one growing inside of me…is *yours*." She emphasized that last word. "I cannot make you accept that, but it is the truth."

He seemed a bit flummoxed. "You were dirty and had paint in your hair that day."

"So that made you assume I was…less?" She might give in to the urge to hit him. "Even if I had been that is no way to treat a woman. There were consequences, and there is a price for that spot of pleasure we found together." It hurt so damn much to say that aloud. Facing him was so hard and she kept fighting the urge to cry. She refused to let him see her hurting so much. "What makes you believe you have the right to use women as your personal toys?" The more she learned disgust filled her. This was the man she'd foolishly fell in love with?

"Because they let me," he said in an irritable tone. "And you were no different, and still aren't, than all the ones that came before you." He sneered at her and his disrespect for her gender flowed through his voice. "You want my title and nothing more."

"I didn't know your title when you seduced me." She glared at him. Francesca *would* hit him before she left. "And I didn't know it until earlier today. It never mattered to me. I'm not impressed with a dukedom."

"Another lie," he said casually. He honestly didn't believe her. "Why else were you there that night? A duke's Christmas party?"

She laughed hysterically. Francesca had never gotten around to telling him about her family connections. He had wondered how often she'd visited Seabrook. She'd never mentioned her grandfather was the Duke of Weston or that her father would inherit that title one day. That Christmastide house party had been at her Aunt Elizabeth's house…the Duchess of Whitewood. In short, Francesca was surrounded by the aristocracy, and high-ranking titles. She wiped a tear from the corner of her eye. "We're a fine pair." She managed to get her laughter under control. "Neither one of us were aware of who each other were. I'm a fool." She met his gaze and told him, "But you, Your Grace, are a bigger one."

"I doubt that." His tone was nonchalant and dismissive. "I'm not the one about to be ruined forever."

"Keep telling yourself that, but you're wrong." She leaned forward as if sharing a secret. "My father and grandfather will ruin you, and if that doesn't work, my uncle will. He used to be a pirate after all."

He blanched at her words. It might be just occurring to him who she was related to. The rumors of Uncle Jack's pirating days were truth, but no one really believed them. "Those are just words. They cannot touch me."

"Because you are a duke?" She grinned with malice shining through her eyes. "It's all right if you do not believe me. I decided you're not worthy of me or my child. I can find someone far better than you." Francesca came to her feet preparing to leave. "But I want you to know one thing…I do not forgive you, and I will be honest with my family now that we've spoken. They will not take this slight lightly."

"I do not care," he said in a flippant tone.

"You will," she promised him. "Because my grandfather is the Duke of Weston and he has far more sway than you ever will." Francesca strolled over to him and leaned down to whisper in his ear. "My father is the Marquess of Blackthorn, and yes, my uncle is the Duke of Whitewood." She stood straight and then tilted her lips upward into a wicked smile. Two could play this game. "You, Your Grace, are now on borrowed time. Enjoy what you have left."

With those words she left him alone to consider his choices. She wouldn't tell her father…yet. He'd call the duke out or something worse. Francesca didn't want to marry him, but it was the best solution for her and the baby. They could maintain separate lives after. If he didn't make an offer for her by the day after her comeout ball, then she'd tell her family.

MATTHEW SAT FOR A VERY LONG TIME IN HIS sitting room after she'd left. He had thought she was high born, but he hadn't realized how connected the chit was, and now he found himself in quite a mess.

He should offer for the girl. It was the right thing to do, and he might not find himself dead after her family came after him. She was right about Whitewood. That one had a look in his eyes that said he'd exact retribution and not think twice about it. Winchester had compromised White-wood's daughter, and now he was married to that chit. They would expect the same from Matthew.

Bloody hell…

Cursing and wishing he could change what he'd done wouldn't help him. He'd told everyone that would listen he'd never marry, and he didn't want to now. Even if she carried his child, he didn't want to tie himself to her forever.

His child…

Something about the idea of his baby growing inside her did odd things to him. He wanted to see her belly get round as his child flourished. He'd already been fascinated by her, but now? He wanted her even more. She'd been so defiant, and bold as she spoke to him. His cock had hardened even more when she dressed him down for the fool he was, and she had been right about that too—he was the biggest arse in existence. He'd never admit it to her though. Matthew should have known about her connections. Most of the guests at that house party had been related in some fashion. Even if she'd been a distant cousin the Duke of Whitewood would not have appreciate Matthew seducing her.

Matthew should never have let her go. He hadn't wanted to believe her, but if she was expecting, the child had to be his. She didn't seem the type to fall into bed with many men. Before he made a decision, he would have to learn more about her. Matthew would not make the same mistake twice. He couldn't allow her to take advantage of him. If his Cesca was telling the truth, his mother would be very happy. Matthew would be able to present her with his duchess and an heir on the way. In many ways that also appealed to him. He could marry her and then dump her with his mother. If his luck held out, she'd have a boy and he'd never have to see her again.

The more time he had to consider it he liked that idea. He would pay a call on the Archbishop and apply for a special license. Matthew believed in being prepared. If he had to marry her, he would have to do it soon. She might start showing soon and that wouldn't do. His duchess had to be above reproach, and he would ensure she stayed that way.

He stood and went up to his chambers. Matthew would need a bath and his best clothes if he planned on visiting the Archbishop. He'd have to bribe the holy man with a lot of funds, but it would be worth it to secure the license. They wouldn't have time to wait. Cesca should have come to him sooner. Perhaps he was being too hard on her there. How could she have? They hadn't been forth-coming with their names. She had probably had to discover his identity and it had cost them both precious time.

He pulled the bell for his valet. "Have a bath drawn." Matthew told him when he arrived in his bedchamber.

"Now?" his valet asked. There was a little bit of shock in the man's tone. Matthew couldn't blame him. He didn't often ask for a bath in the middle of the night. Actually, he didn't believe he ever had before.

Matthew grinned. It was late but he didn't plan on sleeping. He had much to do and not a lot of time to accomplish it all. "Yes, now," he ordered.

"Very well, Your Grace," he bowed and then left to accomplish the task he'd been assigned.

He would have to ask permission to marry her. She hadn't told her family yet about her condition. If she had then it would have been her father, and possibly other men in her family, that had paid a call on him. He could use that to his advantage. It would be better if he had a ring on her finger before they discovered they had anticipated their wedding vows. Once she was his they couldn't do much.

"Your bath is ready," his valet announced.

"Perfect," Matthew said. He'd had a lot to drink, and the bath would help him to clear his head. "Have my clothes pressed. I'm to meet with the Archbishop at dawn." And after that he'd pay a call on Merrifield. He would need a witness at his wedding. "And tell the stablemaster to have my horse ready to depart before my meeting." He should perhaps take a carriage, but a horse would be quicker.

"I'll see to it," the valet answered and left him to his bath.

Matthew settled into the water and leaned back into the tub. He closed his eyes and absorbed the warmth. He was going to be a father. Him. The rogue duke… The ton would be all aflutter with gossip once his marriage was announced. He wasn't certain who would be more surprised: his friends, his mother, or society. Either way, it was the most entertainment he'd had in ages.

Cesca probably thought they were done. She would be in for quite the shock when he paid a call on her. Matthew looked forward to that exchange. Would she be polite or rude? He hoped she'd be rude. He liked it when she thought she had the upper hand. He could not wait to prove her wrong, but what he really wanted was to make her his. He needed her in his bed, at least one more time, and maybe then he could finally erase her from his mind. Matthew prayed that an entire night of her beneath him, living every fantasy he had of her, would be enough.

The sun was high in the sky and warmed Francesca's skin. She held her parasol over her head to block the light from blinding her and overheating her already strained body. She had somehow managed to hide her sickness and crawl out of bed that morning. For some reason her child had decided to take pity on her, at least for one day. She hadn't lost the contents of her stomach, but nausea still filled her. Francesca had skipped breakfast and went to the library to read. Her ball was later that night, and she should be resting. Instead, she was walking in Hyde Park with Violet and Iris. She could not take the chance anyone in her family my overhear what they discussed.

"What did the roguish duke have to say for himself?" Violet asked.

If only she'd know his moniker before she'd fallen into his arms… Francesca sighed. She wouldn't have realized it that night regardless. He hadn't told her his full name. She should have insisted, but she'd been too taken with him. "He denies responsibility."

"Of course, he did," Iris replied, disgust evident in her tone. "He isn't the type that would. Without telling her why I wanted to know anything about him I asked Lady Calliope Andrews. I acted as if I might be interested in him myself." She shuddered a little. "Her brother is one of the duke's closest friends. She has socialized with him often."

"What did she have to say?" Francesca couldn't help her curiosity.

"Not much that we do not already know." Iris frowned. "She believes he had his heart broken once and it has soured him ever since."

"Did he?" She nibbled on her bottom lip. It might explain why he acted the way he did. Still, she couldn't let him treat her as if she were nothing. He had no respect for her or her predicament. She carried his child and he had been far to blasé about the situation. Somehow, he had refrained from physically hitting him; however, she did believe she dealt a much harder blow when she dropped her family name. "Do you know who he supposedly loved?" It did hurt a little to believe he might have had feelings for someone else. The same sort she still had for him and he'd done his best to crush out of existence.

Iris shook her head. "No," she said. "All she could say was she overheard a conversation between her brother, the Earl of Hampstead, and the duke. Lord Hampstead had been berating him about his broken heart, and how he let it rule his decisions."

"How long ago was this?" Violet asked. "I have difficulty believing he has carried these feelings for years. He's been a rogue for quite a while now. Mama keeps telling me to steer clear of him while she still carries avarice in her eyes about the very idea of having a duchess for a daughter."

"On one hand she doesn't want a scandal," Iris began. "And the other is wondering if one of us could turn his gaze long enough to lure him down the aisle." She chuckled lightly. "That's what most of the marriage minded mama's have on their agenda. Ours is no different."

"Except Fran's mother." Violet frowned. "She

never pressures you, and she might be the one to have a duchess for a daughter."

"Mother doesn't care for society rules." Francesca blew out a breath. "And one day she'll be a duchess herself. Why should she bother with pushing me toward a specific title? She would rather I found love than a title he can hold over the heads of the matriarchs."

"That is one of the reasons I adore your mother," Iris said. "She has a reasonable outlook on life. I do wish our mother could follow her lead." She nibbled on her bottom lip. "This will be our second season, and if we don't make a match she'll despair. Two unmarried daughters apparently are the cause for tremendous anxiety…at least for our mother."

"I'd gladly give you my current dilemma in exchange. Either the duke will have to agree to marry me or I'm going to have to find a different suitor, and fast. I'm going to be ruined if I don't find a husband."

"Speaking of the devil…" Violet gestured toward a pair of horses that entered the promenade. One was the duke, and darn it, he looked so handsome it nearly took Francesca's breath away.

"The gentleman with him looks familiar." Francesca said absentmindedly. She didn't care who the other man was because all she really saw was Matthew.

"That is the Marquess of Merrifield," Iris told her. "He's the one Violet has her cap set for, but he never notices her."

"I do not," Violet protested. Francesca glanced in her direction. Was Iris correct? Did Vi have feelings for the marquess. "He probably looks familiar because he was at the Christmas house party too. All the scandalous gentlemen were."

"Scandalous gentlemen?" Francesca lifted a brow. "There were five, but one fell in love at the house party. He married your cousin, Adeline."

"The Earl of Winchester?" Francesca asked. "Who are the others besides the marquess?"

"Your duke is one." Iris grinned. "They are the unattainable gentleman. Every lady hopes to win their heart, but they have other plans, and none of them include marriage. Instead, they leave scandals in their wake."

"Hence the nickname," Violet said. "The other two are Viscount Goodland and Earl Hampstead. We mentioned him earlier."

"Well, they certainly look good on their mounts," Francesca said as she stared in their direction. "It's a pity they're morally corrupt."

Matthew turned in her direction and then glanced at her. The moment he realized she was there she should have turned and gone in the opposite direction. She didn't though. Francesca didn't want to need him; however, she also realized a woman in her position couldn't have the luxury of ignoring him. He motioned for his horse to walk toward her, and his friend followed. Francesca smiled. If her friend did have feelings for the marquess she hoped Violet would forgive her. She was about to flirt outrageously with him in an attempt to make Matthew jealous.

MATTHEW COULDN'T BELIEVE HIS LUCK. HE HAD A marriage license secured, and now his bride-to-be was in the park. He still had to learn some more about her, but he could visit a little with her. It would help him to make a decision. He hadn't yet told Merrifield he planned to marry her or that he had a special license. He was about to tell him about his impending fatherhood, or the possibility of it when he caught sight of her. He could tell Merrifield everything later.

"Where are we going?" Merrifield asked, surprised at their detour.

"I see a lady I must speak with," Matthew said. "It shouldn't take long." Cesca didn't appear too pleased to see him, but he could change her mind. Their conversation last night hadn't ended on a pleasant note, but he'd had time to consider everything. Matthew couldn't let her go, and she'd know that soon enough.

He stopped when he reached Francesca and the other two ladies by her side. Matthew dismounted, the bowed. "Lady Francesca," he greeted. "How fortuitous to find you here."

"Is it?" she lifted a brow mocking him. "Somehow I do not find it so."

Merrifield, who had dismounted when Matthew did, chuckled. "I do believe I like you." He bowed. "I'm Lord Merrifield. Who might you be?"

Cesca turned toward him and tilted her lips upward into a sensuous smile that Matthew wished she had bestowed on him. Why was she looking at Merrifield that way? If she didn't stop soon, he'd have to murder his friend. "I am Lady Francesca Kendall." She gestured toward the other two women with her. "This is Lady Violet Keene, and her sister Lady Iris Keene. It's a pleasure to make your acquaintance Lord Merrifield."

"The pleasure is all mine," Merrifield said in a husky tone. Matthew recognized the shift in his voice. He found Cesca attractive, and at the first opportunity he would discover why that was a bad idea. "Are you enjoying your walk in the park?"

"I am," Cesca said, focusing all her attention on Merrifield. "Would you care to walk with me?"

The hell? "He wouldn't," Matthew said through gritted teeth. He handed the reins to his horse to Merrifield and then turned back to her. "However, I would." He looped her arm with his and forced her to walk with him. He left her companions and Merrifield alone. When they were some distance away, he turned his attention to her. "What games are you trying to play?"

"I'm not the one playing," she said. "Your friend seems nice enough and more worthy of my attention."

Cesca was still angry with him. He would have to soothe her ruffled feathers. He'd been with plenty of angry women. She was no different. "Merrifield is a rake, and you would do well to steer clear of him." He hadn't meant to say that. Bloody hell. What was wrong with him?

She burst into laughter. "And how is that different than you?"

"Matty?" A female said in a throaty purr. "Is that you?"

Matthew stilled. There was only one woman that had ever called him that, and he had hoped to never see her again. Slowly he turned his gaze to meet hers. "Countess Briarton," he said in a cool tone.

"How lovely to see you." She turned her attention to Francesca. "And who is this? A sweetheart? I thought you no longer believed in love." Edith Whitcomb…now the dowager countess of Briarton was as beautiful, and as poisonous as Matthew remembered.

"You do not know me and never did." He hated her and probably always would. He wanted to tell her that despite what she might believe he did not live his life to spite her; however, he couldn't. She had ruined his life and made it impossible for him to believe in love, or that a woman might be telling the truth. It was because of her he'd been so horrid to Cesca. He owned his actions, but he couldn't help wondering who he'd be if not for Edith. He didn't introduce them. He didn't want Edith's poison to touch Cesca or their child. "Now if you'll excuse us, we were enjoying our walk."

"Who is she?" Cesca asked quietly.

"No one of importance," he said quickly. "She is nothing."

"Now who's lying?" She shook her head. The disgust in her tone was unmistakable. "You like to claim it is me, but we both know the truth. Is she right? Are you incapable of love?"

"That is not what she said." That evil woman was already ruining his life again. "She said she thought I no longer believed in love."

"I see," she said quietly. "Because you used to love her and no longer do? Or is it because she still holds a piece of your heart and you hate her for it?"

"I do not love that woman." His tone was a bit harsh, but his feelings toward Edith were not congenial. He didn't want Cesca to think he cared one bit for Edith. "She's not to be trusted."

"Like all women?" She lifted a brow. "I understand."

Matthew didn't think she did. She was staring at him with pity in her eyes, and he did not like it. This walk was not supposed to go like this. She was supposed to fall into his arms, and he could tell her they'd marry soon. Instead, she'd paid more attention to Merrifield than him, and then Edith had to walk back into his life at the most inopportune time. "What exactly do you think you understand?"

"She broke your heart, and you decided that you never wanted to feel that pain again." She sounded intensely sad as she spoke. "It led you to believe breaking mine didn't mean anything. She ruined a part of you, and I cannot allow you to do the same to me." She shook her head. "And that's why it's best we part now. We will only make each other miserable, and I refuse to become bitter like you."

She broke free and walked back to her friends. Matthew let her because she had stunned him with her observation. Was she right? Had he broken her heart the way Edith had his? If so, how could he ever make it right with her?

It was a lovely night, and Francesca couldn't have asked for a better one for her comeout ball. This was her official launch into society, and it would be the last time. She had to accept the truth. Her pregnancy guaranteed she would never be accepted in polite society again. They would snub her, and her child. She'd made her decision and she had to live with it. Her only regret was for her baby. The innocent life growing inside her had never done anything wrong, and he or she certainly hadn't asked for the challenges life would bring.

She wished Matthew had been someone she could depend on. He'd proved to her that he was not a worthy risk. Marrying him would have simplified everything, but it would not have made it all better. He had some demons of his own to face, and she could not be his saving grace. She could barely take care of herself, and she had to think about more than what was best for her. Francesca still wasn't certain she'd made the best choice. She might be miserable with Matthew, but her baby wouldn't have the stigma of being a bastard.

The ballroom was filled to capacity. She was the granddaughter of a duke, and no one had refused an invitation. There would be plenty of gentlemen in attendance. If she had more time perhaps she could convince one of them to marry her. Her dance card was already almost full. Instead of wallowing in self-pity she'd decided to embrace the night. She stood at the edge of the ballroom waiting for her next dance partner. She didn't recall his name and didn't care to. All she could recall was his title, a viscount, no an earl... It didn't matter. He was currently walking toward her with a smile on his face.

Francesca tilted her lips upward hoping that she appeared happy to see him. She needed a break. The ball wasn't as fun as she'd hoped, and it failed to distract her from her dilemma. The entire night had become tedious faster than she could have imagined.

She curtsied when he arrived at her side. "My lord," she greeted. She determined that was a safe enough greeting. "I'm ready for our dance."

"I am glad." He grinned. "But can I interest you in a stroll instead? It's become a bit hot in here."

Francesca did not want to stroll, but as she didn't want to dance either she didn't see any reason to turn him away. "I could use some fresh air." That at least was the truth.

"Then let's go out on the balcony." He led her to the balcony doors. It was nearly as crowded as the ballroom, but there was some lovely light from the moon to illuminate it. She would have preferred the private balcony, but not with him. Perhaps she would escape there after she was done with her allotted time with him. She had another dance partner after him and would have to excuse herself.

"It is a nice night." She sounded like an imbecile. Francesca had nothing to say to him, and quite lost altogether. It was a good thing she was no longer hoping to secure a good match. She would have failed miserably in her endeavor.

"Indeed," he agreed. "It appears spring has finally decided to make an appearance."

He didn't sound all that intelligent either.

Perhaps this was how courtships began… Francesca had no experience to fall back on. When she'd first met Matthew, they hadn't talked this way with each other. It had seemed more natural. This exchange…was wrong. She wanted to escape and never be forced to converse with him again. Which wasn't exactly fair, but it was how she felt.

"We should go back inside," she said abruptly. "I have a partner for the next dance."

"Very well," he agreed. She couldn't tell if he was happy to hand her off to someone else or upset he didn't have more time with her. Either way she was just glad to be done with it.

She breathed a sigh of relief when he left her at the edge of the ballroom to wait for her partner. The gentleman in question was nowhere that she could see. Perhaps she had escaped the impending dance and she could go to the private balcony for a little while.

"You look a little lost," a woman said.

Francesca turned toward her and wished she hadn't. Then she might have been able to ignore her. Now she would be forced to converse with Lady Briarton, the woman who had broken Matthew's heart. "Not at all," she said. "I can hardly be lost in a room I've been familiar with all my life." She hated her. She was the reason Matthew could never really love her.

"You do realize he'll never love you," she said in a callous tone. "His heart belongs to me."

Was she reading Francesca's mind? How could she be so cruel? More importantly, did Matthew still love her? "I don't know what you mean." She would not feed into her beliefs.

"There's no reason to act as if you're unaware of who I speak of," she said in a conspiratorial tone. "I saw the way you looked at him in the park. It's clear you have fallen hard for him. It's best you give up that fantasy. I intend to have him again, and I will not think twice about stomping on you to do so. Don't make the mistake of underestimating me."

"Trust me, I don't." Lady Briarton was a conniving, selfish, harpy that didn't deserve happiness, or to have what she wanted. As mad as she was at Matthew, even he didn't deserve the likes of her. "And you're welcome to him...if he'll have you."

With those words she strolled away from her. She wanted to stomp away in anger, but that would have given Lady Briarton something to sneer after. Instead, she slipped out of the ballroom and went toward the private balcony. She needed a little time alone.

MATHEW HAD OVERHEARD THE CONVERSATION between Edith and Francesca. He wasn't certain how he felt about it. He wanted to go after Francesca, and he would, but first he had to let Edith know she could go to hell. He would never take her back.

"Edith," he said coolly from behind her. "What are you doing here?"

"It's the ball to be at tonight. Why wouldn't I be here?"

"Shouldn't you be in mourning?" he lifted a brow. "Didn't that old man you married die a month ago?"

She laughed, and it had an almost evil quality to it. He wondered what he had ever seen in her. She was beautiful, but there was nothing of substance inside her. "No one expects me to act the loving widow. Everyone knows I married him for his title."

Of course, she had. After she failed to get Matthew to the altar, she'd married the old man. Her reputation was in tatters and she had to do something to repair it. She was also penniless, and the old earl had given her a generous purse. "I suppose that is true." He leaned down and when he was next to her ear he said, "Go home. You're not welcome here."

"Do not be ridiculous. I have an invitation."

He lifted a brow. "I doubt that very much. The Marchioness of Blackthorn would not have sent an invite to a widow of less than a month. I think it is more likely you came with someone that did have one. Go find the fool you convinced to bring you, and leave, or I will have you removed."

"Matthew," she said in a sulky tone. "Is that anyway to talk to the woman you declared you would love forever? We can be together now."

"I was a foolish boy," he said in a dismissive tone. "I had no idea what real love was, and if I did, it died that day. I do not love you and we will never be together again. You are nothing to me." He stood straight and searched the ballroom. His Cesca had left. No matter, he'd find her. "Now do I have to force you to leave or are you going to exit willingly?"

"All right I'll leave," she agreed. "But this isn't over."

"It is," he said in a firm tone. "and if you ever

harass Lady Francesca again, I'll see you ruined, and unwelcome in society. She's to be my wife and I protect what's mine."

She laughed. "Does the little bird know of your intentions?" She lifted a brow. "She didn't seem to care if you want her or not."

Matthew ignored her barb. It hit too close to the heart. He'd handled everything wrong with Cesca, and it was up to him to see it righted. Matthew would marry her, and once she was his wife, he'd have plenty of time to make it up to her. The hard part was gaining her agreement. "You know nothing." He turned on his heels and left her alone. She'd leave if she knew what was good for her.

Matthew left the ballroom and went exploring the Weston townhouse. He'd been there before for balls, and admittedly found a few quiet areas to have some time alone with a lady or two. That was all part of his past. Francesca was his future, and he'd prove that to her. Where would she have gone?

He doubted she would have gone to her bedchamber or the lady's retiring room. She seemed as if she wanted to be alone. Perhaps the library? There wasn't a conservatory there. She could have gone to the private balcony. There were stairs on that one that led to the garden. She liked plants or he believed she did… It was a place to start.

He turned down a hall and then walked to the end of it, then slipped through a door. It was a small room off the balcony. He crossed over it to the doors to the balcony and stepped outside. She wasn't on the balcony, but that did not mean she hadn't gone out there. He went to the railing and glanced down. There was enough light from the moon to illuminate the garden. She sat on a bench near some rose bushes with her head tilted upward as if she were stargazing.

Matthew went down the stairs and headed toward her. When he reached her, she glanced at him and frowned. "What are you doing here?"

"Looking for you." He tilted his lips upward. "We need to talk."

She scowled at him. "You're going to ruin my night, aren't you?"

He wanted to pull her into his arms and kiss her. How could he have stayed away from her for so long. She was perfect, and the exact opposite of Edith. He'd been a fool for far too long. Mathew had made so many mistakes and it would take a while to correct them all. Some he might never be able to fix. "I hope not," he said earnestly. "Will you listen to what I have to say?"

"Shouldn't you go after Lady Briarton?" She lifted a brow "Apparently she's ready to have you in her bed, or perhaps she hopes for marriage this time."

"She always wanted marriage," he said, then sighed. "She used me, and I was happy to let her. I don't want her, and for a long time I didn't want anyone." He sat beside her and lifted her hand into his. "I do want you, and I always have. I was too afraid to trust my own judgement or know what I felt. Please let me have another chance with you. If not for me, then for our child. The baby deserves everything we both can give him."

She lifted a brow. "Are you certain it's a boy then?"

"That would make my mother happy." He grinned. "She wants an heir." Matthew shook his head. "No, I'm not certain of anything. I only want to make you and our child happy. Please let me do that."

She glanced away from him and was silent for several heartbeats. "What do you want from me?"

"Marry me," he said. "I have a special license

and we can do the ceremony immediately. It's the best solution."

Cesca closed her eyes and then said in a quiet tone, "All right I'll marry you." Then she stood. "But I don't want to see you anymore tonight. This is my last night as an unmarried lady, and I'm going to enjoy it." With those words she turned and walked away from him.

Matthew had won this battle, but the war was far from over. She had agreed to marry him, but it was clear she didn't accept there could be more between them than the baby they'd already created. He had a lot to make up for, and somehow convince her that they might find happiness together. If only he knew how to do that…

Seven

She still could not believe she had agreed to marry him. It was a good decision even if she felt as if she'd crumble at the slightest provocation. Her baby deserved to be born inside the bonds of matrimony. The child was innocent of any wrongdoing. If anyone should pay a price it should be her, or Matthew. It didn't matter that he never said he loved her. He claimed to want her and that would have to be enough.

If she wasn't already carrying his child, she might have held out for more. She didn't have the luxury to wait for love. Perhaps over time, after they were married, he would come to love her. Fool that she was she already loved him. Francesca had since they first met. Something had snapped into place when she met him, and it had stayed with her.

He hadn't said when the wedding would take place or where. She should go to see him and discuss it, but she couldn't find the motivation to do so. It was as if once she did it would become more of a reality. Francesca was taking the cowardly way and waiting for him to come to her or contact her in some fashion.

"Lady Francesca," the butler said. "This just arrived for you."

He held a bouquet of flowers—a mix of wisteria and violets. They were beautiful and extravagant. They had to be from Matthew. Francesca hadn't even tried to connect with any of the gentleman from her ball. Her only regret was that she'd never danced with Matthew. She should have insisted he signed her card, but she'd been too shocked by his proposal. He hadn't seemed inclined to offer for her when she'd told him about her condition, and in the park, he'd been too consumed with his former love's presence.

"Can you set them on the table for me?" she said.

"Of course," the butler agreed. He set the blooms on the table and then turned to her. "This came with them." It was a missive. "There was no card." He handed it to her, and then left her alone.

She tore open the missive.

MY DEAREST CESCA,

APOLOGIES ARE NOT ENOUGH, AND I ONLY PRAY IN OUR lifetime I can make things right with you. These flowers remind me of the color of your eyes in the midst of passion, they're not merely blue, but is mixed with all the shades of purple…much like a tempest about to explode upon the earth. You stormed into my heart and broke through the wall I had erected.

Our joining should happen as soon as possible. Please call upon me this afternoon. I've made all the arrangements, and afterward, we can tell your parents together. I do not want to wait to say my vows.

I'M YOURS, ALWAYS.

Matthew

She folded the letter and tucked it away. Francesca did not need anyone to stumble upon it accidentally before she'd married Matthew. He was right of course. They should not wait to say their vows. Their child depended upon both of them to do the right thing.

That didn't mean she wasn't sad. Francesca had dreamed of her wedding day and had hoped that when she said her vows they would be filled with love. The love was there, but it was also mixed with sadness and disappointment. She could not look upon her wedding day as one with joy, and it would always be one founded in necessity.

She had an hour to prepare for her wedding. Should she contact Violet or iris? Shouldn't she have someone she cared about there to act as witness? Resigned she went to her bedchamber and penned a quick note, then went to have the butler deliver it. She couldn't have both Iris and Violet there, and she didn't know if they were available. She asked that one of them attend her and gave them the time and place to meet her there.

Francesca didn't change her gown. She had no special dress for her wedding day and didn't care to change into one of her fancier ball gowns. Besides she would need her maid's help to change, and she didn't want to alert anyone in the household of her plans. She needed the wedding to be finished first. Her parents wouldn't want her to marry without love even though she carried Matthew's child. They would want to her to consider her own happiness, but Francesca couldn't be that selfish.

She took a deep breath and then slipped out of the house. As much as she might like to stall the inevitable, she couldn't. Francesca would arrive earlier than Matthew expected her, but she couldn't wait any longer. Perhaps the wedding could begin early, with or without one of her friends there. She just wanted it to be over with.

The walk to Matthew's townhouse didn't take too long. It was quicker than the first time because she didn't have to stick to the shadows. She strolled up to his door in broad daylight and rapped the knocker against the door as if she belonged there. Soon she would as it would be her house too.

This time Matthew didn't open the door. An elderly man with snow white hair and soft blue eyes stood on the other side. He was probably Matthew's butler. "Yes?" he lifted a brow.

"I am Lady Francesca Kendall. The duke is expecting me." She hoped that Matthew had the foresight to enlighten his servants of her arrival.

"Ah, yes," he said and smiled. "Please follow me."

She entered the townhouse for the last time as an unmarried woman. When she left again, she would be Matthew's wife, and she would have to inform her parent's she married without informing them of her intentions. She hoped they would understand.

The butler led her to the same sitting room she'd informed Matthew of his impending fatherhood. It was different this time. It had been filled with the same wisteria and violets her bouquet had been created with. Matthew was on the far side of the room speaking with a vicar. This was real. It was happening, and suddenly the room started to spin. She was going to faint and there was nothing to stop her, and no one to catch her fall. Somehow that seemed apt…

Matthew glanced over to the entrance of the sitting room as the butler led Cesca inside. He tried to meet her gaze, but she wouldn't look at him She kept staring at the flowers, and then she swayed. He rushed over to her side and barely caught her before she hit the floor.

She moaned and curled against him. "Cesca,

love," he said in a soothing tone. "Open your eyes for me."

Her eyelids fluttered open, but she still seemed a little dazed. "Where am I?"

He titled his lips into a smile. "In my arms where you belong." Matthew brushed a stray lock of her strawberry blonde hair to the side. "Do you think you can stand without swooning at the sight of me again?"

She glowered. "I did *not* fall at your feet."

"In a sense you did," he said in an affable tone. "If you wanted my arms around you all you had to do was ask. I promise I'll happily comply with such a request."

Cesca shoved at him. "Let me up you oaf."

Matthew chuckled lightly. She was all right if she was ordering him around and calling him names. "Gladly," he said. Matthew set her down on the floor gently. "It is our wedding day after all. We have yet to say our vows and I wouldn't want to skip that important part." He stood and then held his hand out to her. "I do intend to make you my duchess today. Shall we?"

She placed her hand in his and allowed him to help her to her feet. Once she was standing, she met his gaze. "I do not wish to skip that part either. It is important to me as well, though I suspect we have different reasons for wanting this wedding to happen."

"I must disagree," he said thoughtfully. "I believe we share the same reasons, but that can wait. The wedding will take place first, then we will discuss the rest later at our leisure."

"Perhaps," she agreed. "But I find I don't much care what your reasons are as long as we're married. The rest is only details and probably not as important as you might believe."

He didn't wish to argue with her about any of it. Matthew wanted the wedding to happen, and if she was in agreement on that much, he wouldn't push her on the rest. At least not yet... After she was officially his wife, he would have plenty of time to explore everything with her. "Then I suppose we should get that tedious part over with. I'm certain saying the vows will not be as painful as you believe. I promise you being my wife will not be a chore you must endure. It'll be quite pleasant."

Cesca rolled her eyes. "I do not need anything of the sort from you."

He winked. "But I do need that from you." Matthew had been dreaming about her, and having her underneath him, ever since the first time they'd been together. He would not abstain from bedding her once she was his wife. It was his right to take her over, and over again, and damn it, he needed her. She was the only woman who haunted him. Edith had never made him feel this much, and he now knew he had never loved her.

Cesca though…she owned him.

"Lady Violet Keene, and the Marquess of Merrifield," the butler announced.

They both entered the room after the butler announced them and they were practically snarling at each other. There was something there between them, but Matthew didn't care to find out. At least not now before his wedding… "Merrifield?" He lifted a brow. "Why are you here?" He never had asked his friend to act as a witness to his wedding. A mistake that can be rectified now.

"I didn't realize I was unwelcome," Merrifield drawled. "The more important question is why is she here." He gestured toward Lady Violet. "And her," he nodded at Cesca. "What exactly am I interrupting?"

"My wedding," Matthew replied casually, and Merrifield flinched a little at his announcement. He'd explain it to him later. "Since you're here you can stand as a witness." He turned toward Cesca. "I assume you invited your friend?"

"I did," she confirmed, then turned to Lady Violet. "I'm glad you could come."

"It wasn't easy," she said, then frowned. "Iris and I had to draw straws to see who would come. I won."

"I'll make it up to her later," Cesca said in a soft tone. Then she turned to Matthew. "We should start."

He nodded. "The vicar is waiting."

Matthew led her over to the vicar. Merrifield and Lady Violet followed behind them. The vicar began the ceremony. They each promised to love, honor, and cherish each other all of their days. The wedding went by in a blur and he said his vows without thinking about them. They were a means to an end, and when it was over, he could have Cesca all to himself. He needed to kiss her something fierce.

"I now pronounce you man and wife," the vicar said. "What God has joined together may no man put asunder." The vicar smiled. "You may kiss your bride.

Matthew almost didn't wait for permission. He'd been tempted to kiss her before the vicar finished speaking. He leaned down and pressed his lips to hers. She gasped and he slid his tongue inside her mouth. This would be no chaste kiss. He wanted to set the parameters of their relationship from the start. They would have a real marriage, and later that night, their vows would be consummated.

He pulled her closer and deepened the kiss. She moaned and kissed him back with equal fervor. This was how it had been between them from the first touch. A fire blazed between them that was undeniable, and constant.

Someone somewhere cleared their throat. Matthew blinked through the haze of passion and managed to pull back. He met the vicar's gaze, and the man winked at him. "It's good to bring two people so much in love together. Since my part is done, I bid you both a good day." With those words the man left them alone. Well, almost alone. Merrifield and Lady Violet were still there, but they could easily be dispensed with. The hell with waiting until later, Matthew wanted to make love to his wife now.

Eight

It was done. Francesca had said her vows and now she was Matthew's wife. Her baby would never know the stigma of being a bastard. There might be talk, but it wouldn't matter. When her child was born it would be within the bonds of matrimony and the date it had been conceived wouldn't matter. Let the whole world talk. She didn't give a damn.

If only she could forget that kiss at the end of the ceremony. Matthew did have a way of making her desire him, and he had not failed there either. The first touch of his lips against hers had sent spikes of desire throughout her. She should have stopped the kiss before the vicar had, but she'd been consumed by him. Matthew was her greatest weakness, and she feared he always would be.

She turned to her friend, Violet, and said, "Thank you so much for being here. It wouldn't have been the same without at least one of my friends to witness the ceremony…what little of it there was to see anyway."

Violet frowned. "I think he loves you."

Francesca shook her head. "I don't believe Matthew knows what love is." She sighed. "I have no doubt he feels desire. That he does understand and uses it like a weapon. He's quite good at it." She placed her hand on her belly. "I know that all too well."

"But you do love him, don't you?" Violet asked in a soft tone. "The way you look at him…"

There was no denying the truth. "Most of the time he makes it quite easy to love him. He can be sweet and attentive." Except for the times he was a complete arse and said all the wrong things. "But it's not enough." It would never be enough… "I'll try to be happy and content with what he can give me. My child has the protection of his name now and that is the only reason I married him."

"I'm sorry," Violet said. Her tone was full of

pity and Francesca hated that. She pulled her into her arms and hugged her tight. "Do you want me to go with you to speak to your parents?"

She shook her head and pulled away from Violet. "No, I need to do this myself. I'm going to go now. Would you walk with me?"

"Yes," she said immediately. "Of course, I will, but don't you want to wait for your husband?"

"He's busy with his friend." She lifted a brow. "About that…" Francesca glanced over at Matthew and Merrifield. "What is happening with you and the marquess?"

"Absolutely nothing," she said. "I thought he was intriguing but now I know the truth. He's an outright bore."

Francesca held back a laugh. She had a feeling there was more than Violet was saying, but it could wait. Violet might say she was no longer interested in the Marquess of Merrifield; however, her constant glances in his direction told another story. Francesca had to get her own life in order before she could become embroiled in her friend's dilemma. When the time came, she would help Violet though. Something told her she would need it. The marquess was part of the scandalous gentleman. Nothing involving them would be easy or simple. "All right," Francesca began. "Keep your secrets. I'm here when you need someone to listen. Now let's slip out while the men are preoccupied." She really didn't want Matthew with her when she faced her parents.

They slipped out and started to walk toward the Weston townhouse. In a couple of days, they were to relocate to Blackthorn house now that her ball was over with. When they reached Violet's home they stopped. "Go on inside. Iris will be waiting for you. I'll pay a call later in the week."

"You'll be over for our weekly tea, right?" Violet asked.

"I wouldn't miss it for anything." She hugged her friend. "Now go before I start to cry. I don't know why I'm an emotional mess."

"You're entitled." Violet stepped back. "It's your wedding day. You only get married once." She smiled. "I do hope you're happy."

"I am." She was in an odd sort of way. All anxiety she had been carrying around with her had dissipated when she said her vows. "Besides I'll have someone else to love soon." The baby growing inside of her would be enough. Francesca would do her best to make it so.

"That's true enough," Violet agreed. "Good luck." With that last bit of encouragement her friend left her alone and went inside.

Francesca finished the trek to her grandfather's townhouse and went inside. No one had noticed she'd left, or at least it seemed that way. She went to the back of the house and into the library where her father had been working until they moved to Blackthorn. He sat at a table looking over ledgers, and her mother was at his side. That wasn't unusual, but something seemed off. "Hello," she said.

They both glanced up when she spoke. Her mother smiled. "There you are. Bess didn't know where you went off to."

"You were looking for me?" Francesca didn't know if that was a good or bad thing.

"Yes," her mother said. "I saw the lovely flowers. Who is your suitor?"

Francesca swallowed hard. This was the part she hadn't been looking forward to. How did she tell them she'd married and didn't bother to tell them anything about her situation? They would still love her. She had never doubted that. She just hated disappointing them.

When she didn't answer right away her mother frowned. "Is it someone you do not favor?"

"It's not that…" It hurt so much. She hated that she worried her mother even for a brief moment. "I…it's just that…" Francesca nibbled on her bottom lip.

Her father stood and walked over to her. "Whatever it is you can tell us. We love you."

That made it even worse. The tears she'd been fighting started to spill and she sobbed so hard her chest hurt. Her father pulled her into his arms and held her tight. "Baby, tell me what's wrong." There was an edge to his voice that Francesca didn't like. "If someone hurt you…"

She pulled back and shook her head. Francesca didn't want him to defend her honor. That was completely unnecessary. "No," she said through the sobs. "I don't need you to rush in and save me. I'm capable of doing that for myself."

"Then tell me what is going on," her father insisted.

Her mother came over then. The color had drained from her face. "My dreams…"

Francesca had forgotten about those. Her mother had been worried about her and had known in some fashion that something was wrong with her. "I'm sorry," she said, and hiccupped. Francesca did her best to rein in her tears. "I never wanted to disappoint you."

"You never could," her father said and cupped her face. "You're our daughter. Tell us what happened."

She drew in a deep breath. "I married the Duke of Lindsey this afternoon." Her mother's mouth dropped open.

"The hell you did," her father said. "That can and will be undone."

"You can't," she told him. She shook her head emphatically. "I have to stay married to him."

"Fran…" Her mother sounded so hurt…

"Why the hell would you marry him without speaking to us?" her father demanded.

"Because she's carrying my child." Matthew stood at the entrance to the library. He looked angry. Francesca frowned and considered perhaps she should have waited for him. "And no one is setting aside our marriage. She's my wife, and she's not leaving me."

It had taken him longer to get rid of Merrifield than he thought it would. When he finally convinced the marquess to leave he realized Cesca had slipped out while he was distracted. Once he realized she was gone he knew where to find her. There was only one place she'd run off to. She should have waited for him. He'd been so angry he had wanted to hit something and found himself wishing Merrifield hadn't already left. He blamed his friend for distracting him.

Now he was in the library of Francesca's grandfather's house facing her parents, and he'd overheard them saying they would have their marriage set aside. There was no way he was going to allow that to happen. Matthew didn't work so hard to convince her to marry him only to lose her now. She was his wife, and that was his child she carried.

Her mother turned toward her. "You're having a baby?"

Cesca face blanched. "I was going to tell you…" She nibbled on her bottom lip. "I just hadn't gotten to that part yet." She glanced at Matthew. "You didn't need to come over."

"The hell I didn't. You should have waited for me." His tone was hard and unrelenting. "You don't need to face anything alone ever again."

"While I find it a little endearing," Cesca's mother began. "You do not need to protect her from us. We would never hurt her."

He tilted his head to the side. "I did not think you would, but it is clear she is upset with something. She's been crying." He wanted to take away all her pain. "What did you say to her?"

"Nothing," the Marquess of Blackthorn said. "She started crying before she told us anything. I have to wonder if it is *us,* she's upset with, or is it perhaps *you*?" He glared at Matthew. "What did you do to my daughter?"

Francesca stepped in front of her father. "Daddy, I don't need your protection. Matthew didn't do anything I didn't want him to."

He wasn't certain he liked the idea of Cesca defending him. She was wrong though. He had taken advantage of her. She'd been innocent and he'd still used her as if she were a whore. He would like to claim he couldn't help himself, and in some ways that was true, but not the whole truth. He could have stopped. Matthew hadn't wanted to. When he first tasted her, kissed her, touched her… he'd become lost to her. When he'd taken her innocence, he should have offered for her then. It was his own self-loathing that had stopped him from doing so. He believed she deserved better than him. It was why she haunted him from that night on. "Love, it isn't that simple." He blew out a breath. "Your father has every right to be mad at me. I took advantage of you, and while I don't regret making you mine it doesn't change the facts. I saw you, I wanted you, and I had you. I should have waited."

"Yes," the marquess agreed. "You should have, and if you hadn't already married Francesca, I'd have made you, then I probably would have killed you. Since you did the right thing without being forced into it, I'll let you live." His lips tilted upward into a menacing smile. "For now." He held his gaze as he said, "You hurt her, and I'll revisit the idea of killing you."

"I'd expect nothing less." Matthew believed he would gladly end his life if he harmed Cesca. "I have no intention of doing so." He looked at the marquess and held his gaze. "I love her." He hadn't realized that he did until that moment. Matthew had known he wanted her, and even needed her, but hadn't realized the depth of his feelings. He turned to Cesca. "I love you. I realize you might not believe that, but I do, and I hope one day you'll love me again."

A tear slipped from the corner of her eye. "You're a bloody fool." She wiped the tear from her cheek. "I never stopped loving you."

She crossed over to him and wrapped her arms around him. He held her close as if he might lose her if he let her go. Matthew was lucky to have her in his life. This entire day was full of surprises. "I'm ready to go home if you are." He wanted to make love to her for the rest of the day. It might be too much to ask, but so far, she hadn't had any difficult granting him his greatest desires. He only hoped that she might continue to do so for the rest of their days.

"In a little while." She stepped back. "I think we should stay and have dinner with my parents. They should be given the opportunity to know you."

He could have argued that point They had a lot of time to become acquainted with him. He had married Cesca after all, and in half a year she'd bear his child, their grandchild. They would have plenty of time to discover the finer aspects of each other. Instead, he nodded. "If that is what you wish to do." He could always love her all night long… He lifted her hand and kissed her palm. "I am yours to command."

She smiled so brightly it made his heart leap with pleasure. "Is that so?" She lifted a brow. "I'll have to keep that in mind for later." She turned toward her parents. "Is it all right if we both stay. I should have asked first."

Her mother nodded. "You're always welcome here." She turned toward Matthew. "You do seem to love her. I hope in time she's not disappointed in her choice." She shook her head. "Sometimes the future is murky, but I believe you two will wade through it with little difficulty." She turned toward the marquess. "I'm going to inform cook we have an addition to dinner tonight. Please don't be rude while I am gone."

"I'm never rude," he replied, then added. "Without cause."

The marchioness chuckled as she left the room but didn't deign to reply. The marquess met Cesca's gaze. "This is truly what you want? I don't care if you're carrying his child. If you want out of the marriage, we can make it go away."

Matthew started to step forward but Cesca placed her hand on his chest. "It is what I want daddy, don't make it difficult." She smiled softly. "I do love him."

"Then I'll let you keep him." He smiled. "Come

give me a hug. It's the least you owe me after denying me the right to give you away at your wedding."

Cesca crossed over to him and hugged her father. "I love you, daddy."

Matthew was choked up. They had a good relationship. It was nothing like the one he had with his own parents. He envied it a little bit, but he mostly felt glad she had them. It meant their own children would have wonderful grandparents through her. They certainly wouldn't benefit from any warmth where his mother was concerned. Though the dowager duchess would be grateful to hear he'd finally married and began siring an heir.

It was perhaps wrong of him, but he hoped their first child was a girl. He smiled at the thought. Yes, a girl would be perfect.

"Are you happy?" Cesca asked.

"Yes," he told her. "I am fortunate to have your love. Nothing could possibly make me happier than that." He pressed his lips to hers. "And soon we'll have a child to share that love with." Matthew pressed his hand to her belly. "I don't deserve you, but I'll be damned if I'll let you go. You're stuck with me."

She laughed. "You might come to regret that one day."

"Never," he promised. He didn't know what love was until her. "Never," he repeated, then kissed her again. Loving her forever was a privilege, and he'd do his best to live up to that.

One month later…

Francesca stared out the window of the townhouse she now called home. The room she occupied would be the nursery. She had decided to spend some time in the room to help her decide how she would like to renovate it. They had to have it completed before the baby was born. So much had happened in such a short time. It was almost too much for her to wrap her mind around.

Matthew had said all the right things in front of her parents, but still she had doubts. How could she not? He'd treated her terribly and suddenly he declared his love? She wanted to believe him, she did, but she still kept a part of herself back. As if she were afraid if she went all in with him she'd only end up a shell of herself. She wanted to make things work with Matthew. She wanted that more than anything.

If not for herself, then for her unborn child. She was now over four months along, and in five short months she'd have a baby. One that would need both parents to be there for him or her. If she couldn't get past her misgivings what kind of life would that be for her child? What kind of life would that be for either of them? She had to be certain once and for all. The problem was she had no idea of what it would take for her to believe in him.

"Cesca," Mathew called out.

She should go find him, and have a discussion. If she didn't tell him how she was feeling and how her uncertainty plagued her, then how could she expect any changes. She was married and had a baby on the way. If there was ever a time for her to be a mature, grown woman, it was now. "I'm in here," she hollered.

Mathew strolled into the room with a large box in his hand. "I know you wanted to wait a little bit before we bought anything…" He held the box up. "But I saw this and couldn't help myself."

"What is it?" She tilted her head. It was a rather large box and she was surprised that he hadn't asked a servant to carry it up the stairs. It looked heavy too.

He set the box down. It was more of a crate really. He pried the wooden top off and gestured for her to come over. "Look," he told her.

Inside the box was a small mahogany wooden horse with a leather saddle on it. The horse's legs were settled on curved wooden pieces similar to what might be on a sled. "A rocking horse?" The baby wouldn't be able to use it for some time. Why had he rushed to purchase it?

"When the babe is old enough it can sit on it and rock like it's riding a horse. Isn't it great?" There was such an expression of happiness on his face… It was breathtaking. Such a simple thing gave him joy. "I know this probably doesn't seem like much to you," he began. "But I didn't have anything like this as a boy. I want my child to know how much we want him or her. I need to be a good father."

Her heart ached. How could she doubt him when he did wonderful things like this? He continued to surprise her all the time. "It's wonderful," she told him. "I don't doubt you will be the best father you can be."

"You don't?" He blew out a breath. "At least one of us has faith in me."

"You should be kinder to yourself. The baby isn't here yet and you already think you might not be what he or she needs. There will plenty of things for us to worry about as our child grows. Your ability to be a father isn't something we need to concern ourselves with."

"I don't think it is that easy," he told her. "But I'll try to relax." He shook his head and closed his eyes, then took several deep breaths. He visibly calmed, but that didn't mean some of that anxiety wasn't still inside of him.

"That's all you can do," she told him. Francesca did love him even when he had been a fool. She looked around the room. "Perhaps that can be our theme."

"What?" he said in a confused tone. "My lack of faith in myself?"

She laughed. "No silly," she told him and then pointed at the horse. "That can be. We can have the furniture made with horses in mind. Have them engraved in the woodwork. Maybe have a mural of horses painted on one of the walls."

"I like that," he said. "I am certain that whatever you decide will be perfect though. I cannot wait to see it when it is finished." His hair was a little ruffled and he had a dreamy expression on his face. He looked like a man in love with his wife and content with his lot in life.

She went over to him and wrapped her arms around his waist and leaned against him. He hugged her and kissed the top of her head. "I love you," he said.

It wasn't a shock as much as it had been in the past to hear him say the words. She was growing more and more accustomed to hearing them from him. Maybe she didn't have to tell him about her doubts. They might be already starting to dissipate. Over time she would grow to trust him more. This was all new and uncertainty should be expected. Shouldn't it?

"I love you too," she told him. She lifted her head and he leaned down to press his lips to hers. It was a soft kiss that spoke of their feelings for each other. Francesca decided her reservations could wait for another today. For now she intended to enjoy being with Matthew.

Mathew sat at his desk in his study going over his accounts. He had even more of a reason to ensure his estates remained solvent. Now that he had a family to consider he was being extra careful. Nothing meant more to him than Francesca and their unborn child. He made sure to tell her how much she meant to him every single day.

He wasn't a fool. Matthew knew she still had doubts. The only thing he knew to do was tell her and show her when he could how much he adored her. Beyond that he had no clue what to do. How could he make her realize he would always love her? He wasn't sure she'd fully accept he loved her, and that wasn't a good sign for their marriage. It was his fault of course. He'd been a right arse from the start. Even the way he'd seduced her and abandoned her hadn't set a good precedent. He didn't blame her for her misgivings. Honestly, he'd have been surprised if she didn't have any at all.

He sighed and rubbed his hands over his face. What the hell should he do. They had been married for five months now. She was due to have their babe in less than a month.

"You look horrible," a man said from the doorway to his study. "Does marriage not agree with you?"

"Hampstead," Goodland greeted his oldest friend. "Why are you here?"

"Can a man not visit one of his closest friends without having a reason?" He lifted a brow. "You wound me." The Earl of Hampstead placed his hand over his chest. "How are you really?"

"I'm all right." He pasted a smile on his face. "I'm worried about Francesca. The babe is due soon and she's grown more and more miserable as each day passes."

"I've heard this stage isn't pleasant for women," Hampstead said. "They're ready to be done with pregnancy." The earl grinned. "I've also heard that they don't want their husbands to touch them ever again too."

It had been weeks since he made love to his wife. He'd feared hurting her or the babe. "I'm sure you're exaggerating." He'd do whatever Francesca wanted. He loved her enough to leave her be if that was what she desired.

"I suppose you'll discover the truth soon enough." Hampstead went over to the decanter of brandy and poured two fingers into a glass. He held up the decanter. "Do you want some?"

Matthew shook his head. "Not right now."

"Matthew..." He glanced up and met

Francesca's gaze. "The babe…it's coming early." She panted as she held her hand to her side. Francesca moaned and held on to the door frame. "We need the doctor."

He turned to Hampstead. Matthew didn't think twice. He set his glass down and met Matthew's gaze. "I'll go for him."

Matthew picked Francesca up and carried her out of the room. He didn't stop to see if Hampstead left for the doctor. His concern was for his wife. When they reached her bedchamber, he settled her on the bed. "What can I do for you?"

"Help me take off this dress." Her breathing was harsh and labored.

Matthew nodded. "Lean forward against me and I'll undo the buttons." She did as he instructed, and with nimble fingers he unfastened them and pulled the bodice loose. Francesca had stopped wearing a corset when it had become too uncomfortable. He had been glad when she had.

He removed her dress, shoes, and stockings. When he was done all that remained was her chemise. "There," he said. "Are you more comfortable?"

"As comfortable as I can be considering," she

told him. Her contractions were coming closer and closer together.

"Let's get you settled in bed," he told her. Matthew removed the quilt and pushed it to the foot of the bed. He settled a sheet over her and then brushed his knuckle over her cheek. "I love you," he told her. "I'm here for you. Just tell me what you want and I'll see that you have it."

Francesca's breathing had grown heavier and it terrified him. He'd never been present when a babe was born. Was this normal? God, he hoped so. He couldn't lose her.

"Don't leave me," she said between breaths.

"I'm not going anywhere," he promised. "I'll never leave you. I need you too much." He kissed her quickly. "You're going to have to get used to having me around. I don't walk away from those I love."

She smiled but he could tell she was still in pain. The hurt was there in her features as she strained against it. "I'm sorry that I've doubted you."

"Shh," he said. "We don't need to talk about that. It doesn't matter."

"It does," she insisted, then moaned as a new wave of contractions attacked her. When they dissipated she met his gaze. "You made mistakes," she began. "But you owned up to them, and since then, you've been a wonderful husband. I…" She leaned against the headboard and screamed as pain hit her. Francesca took several deep fortifying breaths. "I won't doubt you again. I…trust…you."

Matthew stared at the bedroom door. Where the hell was the doctor? What would happen if the babe wanted to come and the doctor hadn't yet arrived. He knew nothing about helping a woman deliver a babe into the world.

"I hear we have a new member of the family coming today," a man said from the doorway.

Matthew breathed a sigh of relief. It was about damn time. He didn't bother responding to the doctor. The man came in and went to work checking over Francesca. "And the little one is ready to come now. It looks as if I arrived in time."

Matthew glared at him. If he didn't need the man he'd hit him. He had such a callous attitude. "It's good you're here then," he said through gritted teeth.

"If you would like you can leave the room. I'll take care of them," the doctor said.

Matthew shook his head. "I'm staying."

"As you wish," the doctor said.

It wasn't long after that a babe's screams filled

the room. Francesca was tired, but she beautiful. She'd always be that way to him. "I love you," he told her. He would never tire of telling her that.

"I love you," she said. "Our baby. ."

"Is perfect," he told her. "Like her mother…" He kissed he cheek. "Rest sweetheart. You've earned it."

Matthew stood and joined the doctor as he checked over the baby. For the first time in his life… he was content. He couldn't imagine ever being happier than this moment. The baby and Francesca gave him purpose. As long as he lived, he'd ensure they were always loved and protected.

Epilogue

It was a warm day. Summer had not yet let go so autumn could take control of the weather. Francesca had been miserable for the entire summer in the later stages of her pregnancy, and she thought she might expire from the heat. Matthew had been wonderful throughout her misery. He'd done whatever he could to help her find some comfort. They had opted to stay in London instead of retiring to his country estate and they were grateful when the baby was born a few weeks early.

That had not made his mother happy though…

The dowager duchess had hoped to be there for the birth of her first grandchild. Of course, she hoped it would be a boy. Francesca only wished for a healthy child, boy or girl. Matthew would need an heir, but they could have more children if the first was born female, and she'd told the dowager duchess that through correspondence.

"Have you written your mother yet?" Francesca asked Matthew. "She should hear it from you about the birth of her grandchild."

"I decided it would be better for her to hear it through the Times." Matthew grinned, and it had an evilness to it. "I made sure to have the announcement sent directly to her."

"You didn't," Francesca frowned. "That's just…wrong."

"She's going to have a fit and you know it," he said. "This way it is more fun." His grin widened. "We might even hear the screams all the way from Lindsey Castle."

Matthew held the baby against his chest and rocked back and forth. The baby was almost a month old now, and they had barely slept since she'd given birth. Their little darling had a set of lungs and was not afraid to use them.

"You are rotten," she told him. "I don't understand why she was so insistent on a boy." Francesca frowned. "She's acting as if this will be our only child."

"In my mother's world it would be." Matthew frowned. "She was grateful I was a boy and then refused to join my father in his bed again. It didn't matter that a spare might be needed. She hated carrying me and refused to do it again when it wasn't necessary." He sighed and rocked the baby again. "My parents didn't have a happy marriage."

"Well, isn't it lucky that we are not them." She met his gaze and smiled. "We can start working on adding to our family once I'm fully healed." She winked. "The doctor said it might me another couple of weeks. I tried to lessen that, but he said if I wanted to enjoy making love to my husband I needed to wait."

"I agree with the doctor," he told her. "I want you in my bed again too, but I won't hurt you." The baby whimpered. "What is it sweetheart. Tell daddy and I'll give you whatever you want."

Francesca rolled her eyes. "Do not start making promises like that now. We'll have a spoiled child on our hands, and then you'll have misery of your own making."

"It will be worth it." He grinned. "I will not be the type of parent that has nothing to do with his children. I'd like a relationship much like the one you have with your parents."

Francesca smiled. Her parents had come to adore Matthew. They forgave him for stealing her away, and not asking permission to marry her. They were ecstatic to be new grandparents. Matthew was taking to fatherhood quite well too, and he often spoke to her father about what he should or shouldn't do. He really wanted to do everything right, and it warmed her heart how much he tried. If she didn't love him before, she would have fallen for him after witnessing him with their baby.

She shook her head. "You are already a great father." She sighed. "However, you're a rotten son. We should visit your mother and let her meet her grandchild. Especially, after the way you are informing her. What exactly did you put in that announcement?"

He walked over to a nearby table and grabbed the Times, then flipped it to the front page. There was a large announcement there.

The Duke and Duchess of Lindsey wish to announce the birth of their first child. They welcome a daughter; Lady Robin August Finley Grant was born the last week of August. She is also the first grandchild of the Marquess and Marchioness of Blackthorn, and the second great grandchild, of the Duke and Duchess of Weston. Lady Robin is loved by her entire family, and they all welcome her with joy. She is a blessing they will cherish always...

Francesca snorted. "You failed to mention she's the first grandchild of your mother."

"I didn't see the point," he said dryly. "My mother wanted a grandson." He smiled down at his daughter. "I personally hoped for a girl. She's too precious for words. Aren't you sweetheart." He cooed at Robin and she blew bubbles at him as if she understood.

Francesca sighed. "Why don't you give her to the nurse. It's past time for her nap."

"Why are you spoiling my fun?" He lifted a brow. "I'm having an important conversation with our daughter."

She rolled her eyes. "That's too bad. I did hope you would take a nap with me." She wiggled her eyebrows. "We might not be able to make love, but I do believe there are other things we can do to pass the time." Francesca sashayed to the doorway. "But if you'd rather spend the afternoon with Robin I understand."

Heat filled his gaze and his mouth tilted upward into a sensual smile. "I won't be long," he promised, and carried their daughter to the nursery.

She laughed as she raced up the stairs, anticipation racing through her. Their relationship hadn't been conventional, but she didn't regret one moment of it. Sometimes easy wasn't always best. They appreciated each other, and their love grew stronger every day. He was her everything, and now they had Robin to make their lives more complete. The announcement had been correct. They truly were blessed, and Francesca would always be grateful for loving her wicked rogue.

Thank you so much for taking the time to read my book.

Your opinion matters!

Please take a moment to review this book on your favorite review site and share your opinion with fellow readers.

www.authordawnbrower.com

Acknowledgments

Special thanks to Elizabeth Evans. Your encouragement and assistance with this book helped me immensely. I am grateful for all you do for me.

About Dawn Brower

USA TODAY Bestselling author, DAWN BROWER writes both historical and contemporary romance. There are always stories inside her head; she just never thought she could make them come to life. That creativity has finally found an outlet.

Growing up, she was the only girl out of six children. She raised two boys as a single mother; there is never a dull moment in her life. Reading books is her favorite hobby, and she loves all genres.

www.authordawnbrower.com
TikTok: @1DawnBrower

BB bookbub.com/authors/dawn-brower

f facebook.com/1DawnBrower

twitter.com/1DawnBrower

instagram.com/1DawnBrower

g goodreads.com/dawnbrower

Also by Dawn Brower

HISTORICAL

Stand alone:

Broken Pearl

A Wallflower's Christmas Kiss

A Gypsy's Christmas Kiss

Marsden Romances

A Flawed Jewel

A Crystal Angel

A Treasured Lily

A Sanguine Gem

A Hidden Ruby

A Discarded Pearl

Marsden Descendants

Rebellious Angel

Tempting An American Princess

How to Kiss a Debutante

Loving an America Spy

Linked Across Time

Saved by My Blackguard

Searching for My Rogue

Seduction of My Rake

Surrendering to My Spy

Spellbound by My Charmer

Stolen by My Knave

Separated from My Love

Scheming with My Duke

Secluded with My Hellion

Secrets of My Beloved

Spying on My Scoundrel

Shocked by My Vixen

Smitten with My Christmas Minx

Vision of Love

Enduring Legacy

The Legacy's Origin

Charming Her Rogue

Ever Beloved

Forever My Earl

Always My Viscount

Infinitely My Marquess

Eternally My Duke

Bluestockings Defying Rogues

When An Earl Turns Wicked

A Lady Hoyden's Secret

One Wicked Kiss

Earl In Trouble

All the Ladies Love Coventry

One Less Scandalous Earl

Confessions of a Hellion

The Vixen in Red

Lady Pear's Duke

Scandal Meets Love

Love Only Me (Amanda Mariel)

Find Me Love (Dawn Brower)

If It's Love (Amanda Mariel)

Odds of Love (Dawn Brower)

Believe In Love (Amanda Mariel)

Chance of Love (Dawn Brower)

Love and Holly (Amanda Mariel)

Love and Mistletoe (Dawn Brower

The Neverhartts

Never Defy a Vixen

Never Disregard a Wallflower

Never Dare a Hellion

Never Deceive a Bluestocking

Never Disrespect a Governess

Never Desire a Duke

CONTEMPORARY

Stand alone:

Deadly Benevolence

Snowflake Kisses

Kindred Lies

Sparkle City

Diamonds Don't Cry

Hooking a Firefly

Novak Springs

Cowgirl Fever

Dirty Proof

Unbridled Pursuit

Sensual Games

Christmas Temptation

Daring Love

Passion and Lies

Desire and Jealousy

Seduction and Betrayal

Begin Again

There You'll Be

Better as a Memory

Won't Let Go

Heart's Intent

One Heart to Give

Unveiled Hearts

Heart of the Moment

Kiss My Heart Goodbye

Heart in Waiting

Heart Lessons

A Heart Redeemed

SCANDALOUS GENTLEMEN BOOK TWO

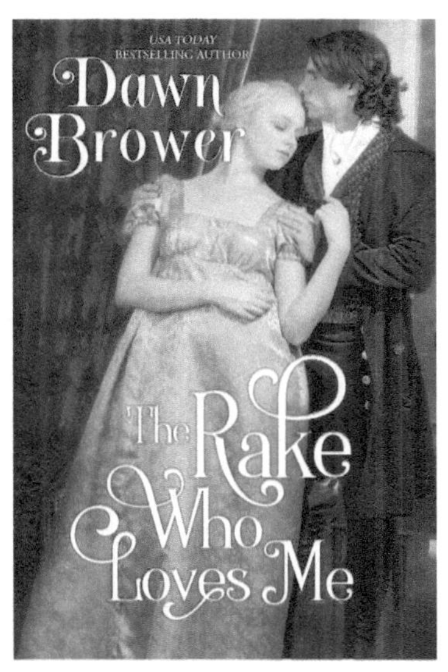

Spring 1866

L ove did not always equal a happy ending...
Lady Violet Keene wanted to believe it did, but she was no fool. The ton did not allow love to bloom. Society had expectations, and love, unfortunately, would never be a part of them. For her, the daughter of an earl, that meant she would have to find a husband. One with a prestigious title and high annual income preferably, but as long as she married, that didn't really matter. The marriage part did.

Today her closest friend, Lady Francesca Kendall, was marrying the Duke of Lindsey. She couldn't be certain if they would have a successful marriage. In the eyes of the ton, Francesca had achieved something many ladies dreamed about. She had made a fabulous match marrying a duke. There would be several disappointed mothers once the news of the wedding spread through the gossip mill. Francesca would have been happier if her wedding hadn't been a necessity. Her friend was in a delicate condition that hastened the need for marriage.

Violet hoped she never made a similar mistake.

A marriage of convenience was not for her. If she had to marry, she wanted something much more substantial than this cold union between the Duke of Lindsey and her friend. Though something told her it wasn't cold at all, but a simmering fire ready to burst. The duke's eyes were heated as he stared at his bride. Perhaps there was some hope for them. They might come to love each other.

Violet glanced at the other person in the room. The Marquess of Merrifield didn't smile. He stared at the duke and Francesca with cold fury. She didn't understand why he seemed so angry, but she wanted to slap him. He wasn't the one being forced to marry. The least he could do was try to support his friend.

She sighed.

The marquess was Violet's weakness. She found him unbearably attractive. Whenever he was nearby, her gaze wandered in his direction before she realized she was staring. His hair was as dark as the night sky and his eyes were a light blue so fair they were almost icy. When his gaze met hers, a chill spread through her. Only he could look at her and make her both heated and frozen at the same time. God help her, she wanted him, but she could never allow herself to give in to that temptation.

The ceremony, what little it had entailed, ended.

Francesca turned to Violet and said, "Thank you so much for being here. It wouldn't have been the same without at least one of my friends to witness the ceremony…what little of it there was to see, anyway."

Violet frowned. "I think he loves you." She wanted to believe that so much, for Francesca's sake.

Francesca shook her head. "I don't believe Matthew knows what love is." She sighed. "I have no doubt he feels desire. That he understands and uses it like a weapon. He's quite good at it." She placed her hand on her belly. "I know that all too well."

"But you do love him, don't you?" Violet asked in a soft tone. "The way you look at him…"

She glanced at her husband. "Most of the time he makes it quite easy to love him. He can be sweet and attentive." There was a wistfulness in her voice as she spoke. "But it's not enough." Her friend craved love from her husband. Violet's heart hurt for her. "I'll try to be happy and content with what he can give me. My child has the protection of his name now and that is the only reason I married him."

"I'm sorry," Violet said. She wished she could make the duke see how much Francesca loved him and that she needed so much more from him. She pulled her into her arms and hugged her tight. "Do you want me to go with you to speak to your parents?"

She shook her head and pulled away from Violet. "No, I need to do this myself. I'm going to go now. Would you walk with me?"

"Yes," she said immediately. "Of course, I will, but don't you want to wait for your husband?"

"He's busy with his friend." She lifted a brow. "About that…" Francesca glanced over at the duke and marquess. "What is happening with you and the marquess?"

"Absolutely nothing," she said. There would never be anything between them. "I thought he was intriguing, but now I know the truth. He's an outright bore."

They slipped out and started to walk toward Violet's home. When they reached Dresden Manor, they stopped. "Go on inside. Iris will be waiting for you. I'll pay a call later in the week."

"You'll be over for our weekly tea, right?" Violet asked.

"I wouldn't miss it for anything." She hugged her friend. "Now go before I start to cry. I don't know why I'm an emotional mess."

"You're entitled." Violet stepped back. "It's your wedding day. You only get married once." She smiled. "I do hope you're happy."

"I am." Her smile wavered a little bit, but she seemed resigned. Violet fought tears. This was all so unfair, and she couldn't help hating the duke a little for hurting her friend. Besides, I'll have someone else to love soon." She placed her hand on her stomach and almost looked serene. Violet hoped that loving that baby would heal some of the hurt.

"That's true enough," Violet agreed. "Good luck." With that last bit of encouragement, violet left her alone and went inside.

She had been intrigued by the Marquess of Merrifield, but after speaking with him several times now, and witnessing Francesca's pain, Violet decided to have nothing to do with him. He was rotten. Much like all of the Scandalous Gentleman. Two had gotten married now, and three remained bachelors. What were the chances they would all fall in love? Violet would hazard a guess of zero. So far only one seemed to truly love his wife—the Earl of Winchester had married Francesca's cousin Adeline. He had been the first of the scandalous gentlemen to fall. The Duke of Lindsey had married, but as to love, that one might never happen.

The remaining three: The Marquess of Merrifield, Earl of Hampstead, and Viscount of Goodland—they would probably ensure they didn't fall into any traps. That was only one reason for her to steer clear of the marquess. The biggest was she didn't want to live her entire life void of love, and he seemed incapable of giving his heart to anyone.

December 1866

Violet stared out the window of the sitting room. Snow floated from the sky in tiny white ice crystals that were gorgeous, even if they were often a nuisance. Winter was far from her favorite season, but she supposed the snow was preferable to rain. At least she could count on the fluffy white flakes from not completely soaking her to the skin. Still...she much preferred the spring and summer months. Snow accumulation didn't allow for easy travel, and she hated being cooped up inside.

"Why are you so melancholy?" Iris asked.

She turned to face her sister and frowned. Iris was her twin sister, but they were not identical. The only thing they shared alike was the same shade of golden blonde hair. Iris had green eyes, and Violet's were a light blue. Today her sister wore a sunny yellow day dress that matched her equally cheerful mood. Violet found it distasteful. Not because her sister didn't look beautiful or that Iris's demeanor was as chipper as a sunny summer day. No, she couldn't blame her sister for her mood. Violet woke up with a sour disposition and nothing seemed to soothe her inner growly beast. She didn't wish to explain herself to Iris, though. It would be long and drawn out, and Violet was already in a surly mood. "Do you ever wish for something so far out of your grasp that it makes you feel as everything in life is impossible?"

Iris sighed. "Of course I do." She stood and walked over to Violet and placed a hand on her arm. "I'm certain we both wish for the same thing too."

Violet doubted that very much. Maybe at one time they may have, but Violet had different aspirations than she had even a few months prior. "What makes you so certain?"

"Because I know you." Iris tilted her head to the

side and then blew out a breath. "You've lost hope, but you shouldn't."

Violet shook her head. "I have not lost hope." She hadn't. Because she never had any to begin with. She couldn't lose something that she never dared to hold inside her heart. "I've decided that I'd much rather live my life with no expectations." Then she'd no longer be disappointed with what she did have. "But today it is difficult to enjoy my blessings." She turned away from her sister and glanced outside. "Especially on such a dreary day." Though she couldn't blame the weather for her mood. Though it provided a convenient excuse...

"You are right," Iris agreed. "On enjoying our life no matter what, and that this weather is dismal." She glanced outside. "Perhaps if the snow lets up, we can go for a walk. We can visit Francesca."

"That's unlikely and you know it." The weather would not cooperate, no matter how much either of them willed it to. Besides, we are to visit Francesca tomorrow for tea. There's no need to go over today." Their friend was happily married with a daughter. In some ways, Violet was envious of that, but she didn't want to be a duchess. She wasn't even certain she wanted to be a wife or mother. Something was missing from her life, though, but she couldn't pinpoint exactly what.

"I wish I didn't agree with you." Iris's cheerful demeanor was slipping. "I had hoped wearing something bright today would help me feel better, and for a while it did, but now..." She nibbled on her bottom lip. "I'm as melancholy as you are."

"Oh, dear..." She met her sister's gaze. "You've caught my doldrums. I'm terribly sorry." She hadn't wanted to inflict her mood on Iris.

"It's not your fault." She moved away from Violet and plopped very unladylike onto the settee. "I've been thinking about Lord Hampstead."

Violet had to restrain herself from rolling her eyes. "That particular earl is not worth any of your time."

Her sister lifted a brow. "Would you say the same if I told you that about Lord Merrifield?"

"Yes," Violet said without thinking. "He's an arrogant rogue who only thinks about himself." That might not be exactly true. He seemed fond of his friends, and he was mostly polite to everyone else. It was only her he seemed to be rude and temperamental with.

"You say that now," Iris began. "But I have seen

how you look at him. If he paid you any sort of attention, you would like it."

She snorted. "Oh, he pays attention to me." Violet paced in front of the window. "He takes the time to tell me everything I'm doing wrong and orders me around as if he has the right to." She clenched her hands into fists. "Sometimes I want to..." She lifted her hands and squeezed the air. "But that would only cause a scandal and I refuse to give into the urge."

Iris chuckled. "I suppose that is somewhere to start."

"Start what?" Violet asked in a startled tone. "You're not suggesting I actually wrap my hands around his neck and give it a good squeeze."

"Well, that wouldn't be a good way to further a courtship along." She shook her head. "But, sister dear, you have his attention. Use it and steer him in the direction you wish to go." She frowned. "At least the man you're in love with is paying some attention to you. "

Violet stared at her sister. "I'm not in love with him."

"Right," she said, then waived her hand. "Keep telling yourself that." She took a deep breath. "We should do something to bring everyone together.

Francesca isn't going to her family's Christmas this year. She doesn't want to travel with the baby. I'm sure there will be others in London."

"What do you propose we do?" Violet was still astonished her sister believed she loved the Marquess of Merrifield. "Have a ball?"

"That's a fabulous idea." Iris beamed. "I'll ask father, and then we can start planning it." She practically bounced out of the room, leaving Violet alone.

What the blazes had she gotten herself into? She hadn't been serious about suggesting a ball. Too late now to take it back, though. Violet turned back to the window and her dismal thoughts. Even the idea of dancing wasn't warming the cold that had settled into her. She feared nothing would...

***

Zachariah strolled into his club. Once inside, he shook the snowflakes off his coat and handed it to one of the workers. He should have stayed home, but he was feeling restless. With the snow falling down, he couldn't go far. Not that he would, but it still limited his options. "Are the Earl of Hampstead and Viscount Goodland here?" He knew Lindsey or Winchester wouldn't be. They were settled at home with their wives and children.

He shuddered at the thought of that domesticity.

The very idea of tying himself to a woman and siring children made him feel ill. He did not understand how two of his friends could have succumbed to the very idea of marital bliss. It almost seemed like a misnomer—marriage did not equal bliss. At least not in his limited experience. Oh, he had never been married before, but he'd bore the brunt of his parent's deep in his soul. They had hated each other to their very cores, and he never wanted to live like they had. He would not marry anyone for any reason.

"Both Lord Hampstead and Lord Goodland are in a private room. They've been here for some time." The man who held Zachariah's coat told him.

"Wonderful," Zachariah said, then grinned. "Then they plan on being here for a while."

"I would believe so," he answered.

Zachariah nodded and walked away to go in search of his friends. He planned on getting foxed and forgetting about everything for several hours. There was only one room his friends could be in. They preferred the room in the far back of the club so they wouldn't be disturbed. The club owners often held it empty for them because they all frequented the club so often. The five of them, the ton dubbed Scandalous Gentlemen, had been inseparable. At least until two of them fell in love... Now there were only three left, and Zachariah hoped it stayed that way.

He stopped inside the entrance and leaned against the doorframe. Goodland was lounging on a leather chair with a decanter of scotch in one hand and a snifter in the other. "Do you ever wonder why we bother with pouring it out of the decanter?" Goodland asked. "When we often drink it faster than we can keep it filled."

Hampstead, who was shuffling cards, answered, "Because we're supposed to be civilized."

"But we're often not," Zachariah said. "Civilized that is."

"It's about time you joined us." Goodland sat up and held the decanter to him. "Come here and I'll pour you two fingers." He lifted a brow. "Unless you want to try your hand at drinking straight from the source."

"For that I think we would need the barrel it came from," Hampstead drawled, then snatched the brandy from Goodland. "Sit," he told Zachariah. "We can play a bit of Faro." He gestured toward Goodland. "He's too inebriated for it to be any fun."

"Is that why you took away his brandy?" Zachariah asked.

"No," Hampstead replied. "I wanted some before he drank it all." He poured brandy into two snifters and handed one to Zachariah, then handed the decanter back to Goodland. "I'd never deprive a friend of brandy."

Zachariah chuckled. His mood lifted a little now that he was with his friends, but he still didn't feel quite right. He wasn't certain what would help, but at least he wasn't completely miserable now. "Are we going to gamble or is this game for fun?"

"Gambling is fun," Hampstead replied. "It would be boring if we skipped that part." He dealt the cards, but neither one of them picked them up off the table.

"What are the stakes, then?" Zachariah asked.

"How about whoever wins gets to make the other do something they don't want to." There was little either one of them wouldn't do.

"That sounds like a challenging task either way." Zachariah grinned.

"I thought it would make things...interesting."

Hampstead lifted his glass and sipped his brandy. "Do you agree?"

"I think we will need an impartial third party." He glanced at Goodland. "To ensure that whoever loses keeps their word, and that the winner doesn't take things too far."

"I'll be your...whatever you called it," Goodland replied with a wave of his hand. "You might need to remind me when I am sober."

"Then we're all agreed?" Hampstead said.

"Yes, we are," Zachariah told him, then picked up his cards.

They played for a while. A servant came in and replaced their empty brandy decanter two times, and by the morning, after hours of play, all three of them were quite drunk.

"There," Hampstead said, as he laid his card on the table. "I win."

Zachariah cursed under his breath. He had lost. There was no arguing the results. "Yes," he agreed, then leaned back in his chair. "The question is: what is it you wish me to do?"

Hampstead grinned. "Nothing too tedious."

That didn't sound good at all. "Then why do I believe otherwise?" He lifted a brow.

"Because you're a suspicious person." Hampstead finished the brandy in his glass.

"I have had plenty of reasons to be." His parents hadn't left a good impression on him as a child and it spilled heavily into adulthood. "So, tell me."

Hampstead sighed. "Fine. I've had most of the night to consider what I would ask of you." He lifted the empty decanter and stared at it, then set it down. "I don't need anything from you, but you do need to do something for yourself and you never will unless someone makes you."

Zachariah had a terrible feeling settling inside his gut. He had made an error and he could not back out of it. This was a debt of honor, after all. "What," he nearly growled the word out.

"I want you to," he paused. "Not court a woman. That's asking too much, but... become acquainted with one. Talk to them and learn something personal about them. Their likes, needs, wishes...outside of a bedroom. I don't mean a courtesan or actress, but a proper lady. One that any of us could be seen with in public." Merrifield folded his hands together. "And Goodland and I will choose the lady for you."

Zachariah cursed. "How long do I have to complete this task?"

"By the end of Christmastide," he answered. "We shall choose the lucky lady for this endeavor sometime later today." He winked. "We'll need to rest a bit first, but we wouldn't want to keep you waiting for long."

"All right." He wanted to punch something, but he refrained. Lucky lady indeed… Zachariah didn't believe this unknown paragon would feel fortunate, but perhaps he was wrong. She might think he intended to court her and if so that would be disastrous. "If you'll pardon me. I think it is past time I returned home." Without another word, he stood and turned away from his two friends. The night had been pleasant until his friend stabbed him straight in the heart. This was a betrayal he would not soon forget, and he'd ensure that, in some fashion, Hampstead would pay for making him do this.

Excerpt: Courting a Christmas Wallflower

CHRISTMAS WALLFLOWERS BOOK 12

Christmas Wallflowers

Courting a Christmas Wallflower

USA TODAY BESTSELLING AUTHOR

Dawn Brower

Prologue

Lightening flashed moments before thunder struck and rattled the windows of Evangeline Payne's bedroom. She shook beneath her blanket. Eva hated storms, but loud ones always made her nervous. This storm was no different.

Her mother, Daphne Atwood Payne, Viscountess Norwich had died during a storm like this one. That was four years earlier when Eva was three and ten. It was then when she'd become timid and lost the ability to speak well in polite company. Storms had become her greatest weakness.

Her father had changed after her mother's death too. He'd become distant and angry. His temper flared at the slightest provocation. Her stammer hadn't helped when he wanted her attention. She tried to avoid him at all costs. She relished the moments when she was allowed to visit her grandmother, Theodora, the Dowager Countess of Birchwood. At her grandmother's estate she felt free, but still even there with her three cousins for company she couldn't shake the stutter that plagued her.

She was going to stay with her grandmother in a week and she couldn't wait. The storm only made her more anxious. What if it was an omen of sorts? If her father forbade her from going Eva didn't know what she would do. She had to go. She just had to.

Eva slipped out of bed and made her way to the window. She should face her fear and maybe then she could lose the stutter too. Something had to change or she would never be able to escape her father's house. She needed to marry, and she prayed for something to help her do that.

Her hand shook as she opened the window. With it wide open wind blew inside and the rain pelted against her skin. She lifted her head and let it pour over her face. The pain that prickled her skin from the drops of water was enough to shock her to reality. This was silly. Another flash of lighting and the pound of thunder rattled around her. Eva took a deep breath and then stepped away from the window. She was tired of being afraid.

She stared at the stormy sky and made a promise to herself. This summer when she was at her grandmother's estate, she would make a change. She would become a woman a man noticed, and she would find a husband. If she couldn't do that, then she had no real chance of a future. Her father drank too much brandy and he got meaner the more foxed he became.

Eva was tired of being afraid of her own shadow. It was time to live in the light. She stepped forward and closed the windows. Storms were not going to be her weakness anymore. Instead the tempest would be her strength as she walked into the storm and faced everything it threw her way.

She slipped into bed again and settled beneath her blanket. For the first time in a long time she slept peacefully. As if fate had given her a gift. One she had been waiting for and hadn't realized it. All she had to do was accept it and her greatest desire would be hers. Finally.

Order Here: https:// books2read.com/CourtingWallflower

www.ingramcontent.com/pod-product-compliance
Lightning Source LLC
Chambersburg PA
CBHW021000180726
47993CB00017B/400